'How did she get in here?' he demanded of Lisa.

'The lady has a key. You appear to hand them out like candy bars at Hallowe'en. But don't let me interrupt. I'll just get my things and go.' She headed for the dressing room, but Alex stopped her. He had leapt out of bed stark naked, and now grabbed her by the shoulders.

'Don't be ridiculous, Lisa, this is all a terrible mistake. Surely you can see that?'

'I can see everything,' she snorted, 'and so can your lady-friend. But then there's nothing she hasn't seen before.'

Alex let fly with a string of curses in Greek, while grabbing the sheet from the bed and wrapping it around himself. Free of his hold, Lisa headed for the door.

'Not so fast,' he growled, and caught her arm. 'You must have seen her come in here. Why didn't you stop her? You're my *wife*, for heaven's sake.'

'Was,' she said trenchantly...

GREEK TYCOONS

Men who have everything—except a bride

Wealth, power, charm—what else could a
heartstoppingly handsome tycoon need?
Meet Dio, Constantine, Alex and Andreas,
four gorgeous Greek billionaires who are each
in need of a wife.

From January to April, each month one of these tycoons
meets his match and decides that he *has* to have
her...*whatever* it takes!

Look out next month for
THE TYCOON'S BRIDE
by Michelle Reid.

HUSBAND
ON TRUST

BY
JACQUELINE BAIRD

MILLS & BOON®

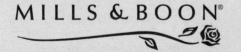

First published in Great Britain 2000
Harlequin Mills & Boon Limited,
Eton House, 18-24 Paradise Road, Richmond, Surrey TW9 1SR

© Jacqueline Baird 2000

ISBN 0 263 81964 7

Set in Times Roman 10½ on 12 pt.
01-0003-55124

Printed and bound in Spain
by Litografia Rosés, S.A., Barcelona

CHAPTER ONE

LISA raised her hands above her head, stretched, and yawned. With only a fine cotton sheet covering her body she felt decadent and deliciously languorous, due entirely to the expert administrations of her very new husband last night.

The door to the *ensuite* bathroom opened and Lisa's gaze automatically turned to the man walking into the bedroom. Six feet plus of pure masculine perfection, he was naked except for navy silk boxer shorts hugging his lean hips. He was also strikingly handsome, his strong dark features cast in the classic mould of the Greek male of legend, and he was hers, Lisa thought on a swift, involuntary breath. His thick black hair was still damp from the shower, a stray droplet of water easing its way down his strong throat and lower, to be captured by the curling black body hair that dusted his broad chest.

A lazy smile curved her full lips. 'Alex,' she said softly. Just saying his name was a pleasure. Sometimes she felt like pinching herself to make sure the last few weeks had not been a dream.

In the process of pulling on a crisp white shirt, he turned his dark head and his eyes clashed with hers. 'I know that tone of voice, wench, but forget it. I have to be in London by eight-thirty.' He grinned and continued dressing, stepping into grey tailored trousers.

'Spoilsport.' She pouted, and moved across the bed, allowing the sheet to slip to her waist. 'Do you have to leave so early?' she queried huskily, and was rewarded by Alex's renewed attention. He walked over to the bed and, bending down, brushed his mouth over hers; her lips parted, hoping to prolong the kiss, but abruptly he straightened up.

'Not this morning, Lisa, I have no time.' And, turning, he crossed the room, picked up his jacket and eased himself into it. 'I told you that yesterday, when we drove up here. Today I have meetings lined up in London, morning, afternoon and late into the evening,' he flung over his shoulder, as he picked up his wallet and keys from the dressing table. 'And from what your stepfather said last night, you have a busy day ahead of you.'

Lisa sighed; Alex was right. They had arrived back in England last night and travelled straight to her home in Stratford-upon-Avon. On the death of her mother nine months ago, Lisa had inherited the major share in the family company, Lawson Designer Glass and her mother's job as managing director. Her stepfather, Harold Watson, was the marketing director.

'You're right; I know,' Lisa grudgingly conceded, and, sitting up, she swung her long legs over the side of the bed. She grasped the sheet and wrapped it around under her arms, sarong-style and stood up, flicking a glance at Alex as she did so.

'Amazing! You hide yourself in a sheet.' A dark brow rose quizzically. 'I have seen everything many times, no?' he drawled, and, turning his back on her, he picked up a silk tie, and slipped it under his shirt collar.

Lisa hesitated and, realising how ridiculous it was to cover herself in front of him, she let the sheet fall to the floor. A month ago she would have died if any man had seen her naked, but Alex had cured her of almost all her inhibitions. Her gaze lingered on his broad back; the exquisitely tailored jacket hung perfectly off his wide shoulders, the few tendrils of black hair curling over the collar an endearing dent in a picture of sartorial elegance, she thought with a grin. At that moment Alex turned back round and caught her staring.

His deep brown eyes flared for an instant, as his glance swept her from head to toe. Lisa was a tall girl, five feet nine inches, but perfectly proportioned, with high, firm breasts, a narrow waist, slim hips and legs that went on for ever. The three weeks of their honeymoon, which they had spent sailing around the Mediterranean on Alex's yacht had given her skin a golden glow, the sun adding natural streaks of platinum to her long blonde hair.

'I guess the honeymoon is over and work beckons for both of us,' she said huskily, hiding a smile. She could tell he was rethinking the need for an early departure. From the moment she had met Alex he had awakened a sensuality in her twenty-three-year-old soul that she had not known she possessed. She had taken one look at him in the lounge bar of a local hotel and had fallen in love on the spot. It had been the same for Alex; they'd spent the next day together and by the evening he had proposed marriage. She would have slept with him there and then, so overwhelming was the passion she felt for him. But Alex, with iron self-control, had insisted they wait until they were married. Four weeks later they had been. Her wedding night had been a revelation: Alex was the perfect lover—he had fulfilled all her wildest dreams, and then some!

'I have a feeling our honeymoon will never be over,' Alex declared throatily, and, stepping towards her, he lifted his hand to stroke the soft curve of her cheek. The simple touch was enough to make her pulse race and her stomach clench with excitement. His dark eyes holding hers, his hand trailed tantalisingly down to her shoulder and traced over her breast and waist before hauling her hard against his long length, his head sweeping down to capture her mouth with his own. The kiss was deep and devouring, and when it ended Lisa stared up at him, totally enslaved, her heart bursting with love for him.

'But for today it is,' he added, letting her go. 'We don't have time to discuss it now, but you are going to have to sort something out about Lawson's. I want you with me, Lisa, not tied to a desk.' He paused. 'Well, not unless it is my desk,' he qualified, his dark eyes dancing with wicked amusement.

'Naughty man!'

'It is not me who is stark naked!' he drawled mockingly and, with a swift pat on her derriere, he added, 'Go shower, and I'll go make the coffee.'

Ten minutes later, having showered and wearing a long blue towelling robe, Lisa strolled into the kitchen of the elegant ten-roomed house that had been her home for as long as she could remember. Alex was leaning casually against the worktop, a coffee cup in one hand, a mobile phone in the other, talking in rapid-fire Greek. He glanced across at her as she walked in and indicated the coffeepot with a wave of his cup, but didn't stop talking.

Lisa poured herself a cup of coffee and sat down at the breakfast table, her blue eyes lingering on his rugged profile. His black hair was swept back from his broad forehead; thick black eyebrows arched over deep-set brown eyes; his nose was a straight classic line and his mouth a sensual invitation—perfectly sculptured lips, the bottom one slightly fuller than the top. But at the moment, they were tight with anger.

The honeymoon was certainly over. Alex Solomos the entrepreneur was back. Lisa knew he was the owner of a large company, Solomos International, which his father had started as a small construction firm in Athens. But since Alex had assumed control the company had expanded into a variety of different interests worldwide, all successfully.

Taking a sip of her coffee, it struck Lisa quite forcibly that although he was her husband she did not really know a lot about the man she had married. He was Greek, an only child. Alex had told her that his parents had divorced when he was seven and his father had married again and again, almost wrecking his business in the process. Until Alex had stepped in and taken control after the third divorce, insisting his father must make a prenuptial agreement in any future marriage. Two more marriages had ensued, which was why, Alex had explained, *they* must have a prenuptial agreement. He could not have insisted on his father doing so and then refuse to do so himself. Lisa had agreed, and had quite happily signed on the dotted line.

Lisa had met his mother on her honeymoon, when Alex had berthed the yacht in the harbour at Kos and they had spent the night in a luxurious villa overlooking the sea with the elegant silver-haired woman. In her halting English she had told Lisa Alex was named after Alexander the Great. The old lady had explained her family was partly of Macedonian descent, the same as his namesake, a man who had conquered the whole of the known world centuries ago, including the island of Kos.

A vivid mental image of Alex, his naked body entwined with hers on the large bed in the villa, flooded her mind. She had teased him about Alexander the Great. 'I hope you don't take after the man in every respect, because, according to most historians, although the man was married he was gay.'

Alex had responded with, 'Then I must prove otherwise, wife,' and had proceeded to make love to her until they were both satiated by passion. Afterwards she'd quite happily conceded he *was* great, in at least one department...

Thinking about it now brought a dreamy smile to her lovely face. She lifted the coffee cup to her mouth and drained it, her glance straying once again to Alex's long body. She could easily see the connection. He was a stunningly attractive man, and with the same type of ruthless energy and drive that conquered worlds. Which, when she thought about it, made it all the more amazing that he had fallen in love with her and married her... In the last three weeks Alex had introduced her to the world of the senses, as well as to the sophisticated lifestyle of some of his wealthy friends.

Suddenly he clashed the phone down, and Lisa's eyes widened at his thunderous expression. 'Bad news?' she asked.

'My father.' He strolled towards her, running a hand through his thick black hair. 'But nothing for you to worry about.' He dismissed her enquiry with a shake of his dark head. 'I must leave. It is a two-hour drive to London, providing the traffic is not snarled up. I don't have time to waste.'

Lisa stood up and slipped her arms around his waist, the familiar warmth of his body, the husky male scent of him making her heart flutter in her breast. 'I'll see you tonight.'

He glanced down at her upturned face, a wry smile curving his firm lips. 'No. My last meeting is scheduled for seven-thirty this evening, and tomorrow morning I have an eight o'clock breakfast meeting. You stay here, pack what you need, and have it sent to the London apartment. We will make that our base for now. But we will have to discuss something more permanent. Get your own work up to date and then I suggest you consider employing someone to take your place. Talk it over with Harold. You seem to be fond of your stepfamily. Something I've never managed to achieve,' he concluded dryly.

'Yes, yes, I am. Harold worshipped my mother, and he has always been brilliant with me. But...' She got no further.

'Good,' Alex cut in. 'Spend the evening with him; he will be glad of your company.' His dark head bent and he brushed the top of her head with his lips, before curving his hands around her upper arms and putting her away from him.

Lisa was not sure she liked the arrangement. The thought of even one night without Alex was hard to bear. Although she knew it made sense. 'Are you trying to get rid of me already?' she tried to tease. But she realised Alex was already gone, if not in body then certainly in spirit.

'No. But I have neglected business long enough. As long as you work, we are going to have to get used to spending time apart. Not desirable, but in the present circumstances inevitable.' And, slipping his hand into his pocket, he withdrew a bunch of keys and removed one. 'Here is a key to the penthouse. I will inform Security to expect you.' He handed her the key. 'I'll see you tomorrow.'

'Yes.' Lisa had only been to his apartment once, on their wedding night, when Alex had introduced her to the joys of love for the very first time. She would have reminded him but he didn't give her the chance.

He glanced at his gold Rolex. 'I must go. Make sure you are in London by six tomorrow night, Lisa. We are dining with my father at seven thirty.' And, with a brief kiss on her open mouth, he spun on his heel and walked out. Lisa followed him into the hall, in time to see him open the front door and disappear through it without a backward glance.

'Was that the door?' a gruff voice queried from the top of the stairs.

Lisa turned around 'Yes, Harold.' She smiled up at the elderly man descending the staircase. 'Alex has just left. Give me ten minutes to get dressed and then I'll get breakfast.' Running lightly up the stairs, she gave her stepfather a little peck on the cheek as she passed him.

Later, when the two of them sat side by side at the breakfast table, the bacon and egg Lisa had cooked long since eaten, they lingered over their coffee, talking about work.

'Mary, your PA, has been wonderful,' Harold said firmly. 'In fact, no disrespect to you, dear, but I think the woman could almost handle your job.'

'Thanks very much. Glad to know I was missed,' Lisa drawled mockingly.

'I didn't mean it like that, Lisa, but you are very much a new bride, and your husband has to come first. You should be at Alex's side, not sitting here with me.'

'Yes, I know. Alex said pretty much the same. As it is, I won't see him until tomorrow—pressure of work...' She shrugged her shoulders and, with a rueful smile at Harold, she pushed her chair back from the table and stood up. 'Tonight I'll be dining with you but right now we'd better get to the office.'

They took Harold's car, a blue Jaguar, and after pulling up in the courtyard of Lawson Designer Glass, Lisa slipped out and viewed her surroundings with a contemplative air. The firm had been the brainchild of her parents. She remembered her mother describing to her how she had met Peter Lawson at a dance in Oxford, and had fallen in love on the spot. He had been the only child of the main partner of the Lawson Lee Glass Factory in Stratford-upon-Avon, a long rambling place that sat alongside the river. Her mother had been an accountant. They had married, and by the time they were thirty, and Lisa had arrived, her grandfather and the silent partner Lee, had died.

Her parents had transformed the factory into one of the leading producers of Tiffany lamps and designer glass in Europe. The Lee heirs had had no interest, other than the twice-yearly dividend, and had made no objection to the change of name to Lawson Designer Glass. Her mother had looked after the financial side, and her father, the more artistic, had simply loved designing. Unfortunately he had died in a car crash when Lisa was nine. Two years later her mother had married Harold Watson, a man who had worked for the firm as sales manager for several years and was a true friend.

Lisa had worked here in the school holidays, and then after graduating from university full time. She loved the place; it had been her whole life so far, but now she had Alex. Juggling a husband and a business would be no easy matter. There were going to have to be some changes.

In fact the changes had already started with the death of her mother last year from stomach cancer. Three short months after the diagnosis her mother had been gone. But when she was dying she'd confided in Lisa; she had loved Peter completely, they had been soul mates, and she had thought it her duty to carry on with his work after he died. Her marriage to Harold, she'd admitted, had not been built on the same kind of love.

Harold had been alone ever since his first wife had left him with a small son to look after years before. That small son had been a twenty-seven-year-old man, with his own

commercial estate agent business in London, by the time
Lisa's mum had married Harold. As her mum had later
confessed, it had been more for companionship than love
on her part, but she had hoped Harold would be a good
father figure for Lisa.

In that respect her mother had been right. Lisa adored
Harold, and the brief visits of his son Nigel had not really
impinged on her life. Except for the year when she was
sixteen and Nigel had made a pass at her. But, as she'd
already been a big girl, she had quickly disabled him with
a hard knee to the groin, and it had not been a problem.
On the subsequent rare occasions they had met they'd
managed to uphold a polite façade.

Smoothing the fine linen of her short skirt down over
her hips and adjusting the collar of her jacket, Lisa entered
the building, a worried frown pleating her brow.

Her mother had died in Saint Mary's Hospice, and her
dying wish had been that five per cent of Lawson's be
gifted to the hospice. She'd had no time to change her
will to encompass this, so Lisa had received fifty-two per
cent of the company, and Harold had got the house. He
also owned thirteen per cent of the company—shares he
had accrued in bonus payments over the years in a scheme
her father had set up. The will had passed probate the
week before Lisa had married and against her better
judgement, she had done as her mother requested the
Friday preceding her wedding. The trouble was, she had
yet to tell Harold, because she knew he would have insisted on making the donation himself. But realistically
she could not see it being a problem as between them
they still controlled the company. Now, Lisa had no more
time to dwell on the subject, as various members of the
staff greeted her return with huge smiles and a few sug-
gestive remarks.

Mary was already in the office when Lisa walked in. A widow of forty with two teenage children, she had worked for the firm for seven years, and as Lisa's PA for the last year.

'Welcome back,' Mary said, looking up from behind her computer terminal. 'I won't ask if you had a good honeymoon; I can see it in your face.' She grinned.

Lisa had invited all the workforce to her wedding. It had been a traditional service in her local church on a Monday afternoon. The reception afterwards at Stratford's leading hotel, apart from the fact that the best man had taken off immediately after his speech, had been a great party. Lisa and Alex had finally left late in the evening to spend the night in Alex's London apartment, before flying out to Athens the next morning to board his yacht at the port of Piraeus. Thinking about it now brought warmth to her cheeks.

'Yes, it was very nice,' Lisa responded primly, and then winked. 'My husband is all that, and more!' Crossing the room, she lingered for a moment at the picture window, glancing at the view of the River Avon and fields beyond. It was a clear, blue-skied June day. A day for lovers to take a picnic and explore the countryside hand in hand. 'And why I am here working when Alex is in London, I do not know,' Lisa said out loud, before sitting down on the chair behind her desk and glancing up at Mary. 'I must be mad.'

'Madly in love,' Mary quipped, placing a sheaf of papers on Lisa's desk. 'Priority messages, okay?'

Two hours later, musing over a cup of coffee, Lisa realised that Harold was right, all the work was up to date except for a few items that demanded her personal attention.

'Congratulations, Mary, you've done a great job in my absence,' she surprised the other woman by remarking.

Mary beamed back at her from her desk. 'Thank you. It's good to know I'm appreciated, but can I ask you something?'

'Sure, ask away.'

'Well, there have been rumours, now you're married…' Mary hesitated. 'Well, rumours you might sell up.'

'I promise you, Mary, the rumours are completely without foundation. In fact, I was about to ask you if you would like to take on more responsibility. A promotion; doing what you have been doing the past three and a half weeks. Obviously we'll hire someone else to take over a lot of your existing work. And it would mean a substantial increase in your salary.' Lisa mentioned a sum more than double Mary's present salary. 'Does the notion appeal?' Lisa asked, grinning at the stunned look on Mary's face.

'Appeal? I would love it.'

'Then get on to the agency and see if you can set up some interviews for Monday, for someone to replace you.'

'But what about you?' Mary asked. 'I mean, you love your work.'

'Oh I'm not giving up all together. But, let's face it, most of the work I have left to do today could as easily be done from my laptop at home, or wherever Alex and I happen to be.'

'Which reminds me,' Mary chuckled. 'Have you checked your E-mail since your wedding? I've had a couple of messages from a Jed Gallagher in Montana on the office computer which were obviously meant for you.'

Lisa grinned from ear to ear. 'Jed! I must get back to him.'

'Don't forget you're a married woman now,' Mary reminded her. 'Alex Solomos might be drop-dead gorgeous, but you know what they say about Latin types. Jealous to the bone. What would he have to say about your on-line romance?'

'You don't understand.' Lisa grinned at her assistant. 'Jed is nothing like that. He's almost like a brother to me. I can remember the first time we linked up. Mum had bought me a new computer for my eighteenth birthday, and I got on-line. One day, whilst flicking through a list of subscribers to one of the chat rooms, I came across Jed. His profile said he was tall, blond, nineteen, and lived on a farm in Montana. I sent him an E-mail and he replied the next day, and that was it. We've been mates ever since. I can confide my deepest thoughts to him and he responds in kind. But it's completely platonic, and as for Alex minding—the man hasn't a jealous bone in his body.'

Something Lisa had been made very aware of the second week of their honeymoon.

They had berthed in Monte Carlo for the night and Alex had taken her to a glittering party on the yacht of a friend of his father's. They had been dancing on the deck to the music of a well-known quartet when a man had cut in and, much to Lisa's chagrin, Alex had agreed with alacrity. Seconds later she'd been in the arms of an overweight man, who had to be sixty if he was a day. And, looking over his shoulder, she had watched Alex talking apparently very seriously to a sultry eyed, black-haired woman, whom Lisa had thought vaguely familiar, until her partner had enlightened her: Fiona Fife, a model, who'd been staying on his yacht till the weekend.

No, if anyone suffered from jealousy, it was herself, Lisa thought moodily.

'Cheer up, girl, it might never happen.' Harold's voice cut into her thoughts as he walked into her office. 'I'm taking you out to lunch.'

'There's no need. I'm having dinner with you tonight, remember?'

'No you're not! I've been thinking about it all morning. You staying here tonight while Alex is in London. It's not natural for a newly married couple.'

'It's pressure of work, Harold.' Realistically Lisa knew she would have to get used to spending days at a time without her husband. His business took him all over the world. He had offices in New York, London, Athens and Singapore. And they had not really discussed yet where they would eventually settle down.

Lisa chewed on her bottom lip, her blue eyes troubled. For three weeks they had done nothing but make love, eat, sleep, and occasionally party, in the few ports where Alex had bumped into friends. Today they were back in the real world, and look what had happened: they were apart.

'Rubbish, Lisa!' Harold remonstrated. 'Mary can manage.' And, turning to Mary, he commanded. 'Get on the telephone and book a seat on the five-thirty train to London.' Then, turning back to Lisa, he added, 'Food first, and then we'll discuss your future working arrangements.'

'Actually, I already have—with Mary. I've offered her a promotion,' Lisa informed him with a smile.

'There you are, then. Give that husband of yours a nice surprise.'

The idea was tempting. Alex had made all the running in their relationship. Only this morning he had teased her about still being shy because she'd had the sheet wrapped around her. Perhaps it was time she showed him she could match him for sophistication. She could let herself into the apartment, slip on her sexiest negligé and seduce him when he got back from his meeting. Just the thought made her stomach tremble, an impulsive action, but why not?

'I'll do it,' she declared firmly, and felt her colour rise at the knowing looks Mary and Harold gave her. Leaping to her feet, she added, 'Book the seat, Mary, and come on, Harold. If you're taking me to lunch let's go.'

After lunch, Lisa did some shopping, and then went back home and packed her bags. Finally, before leaving for the station, she spent half an hour on her laptop, E-mailing Jed. He told her he was back home for the summer after completing his fourth year at college. She was glad for him, because she knew he'd had quite a fight with his brothers to even get to college; they had not approved and had wanted him to stay on the farm. She told him all about the wedding and the honeymoon, and grinned at his last reply.

'Your marriage sounds as if it's made in heaven, as does your husband. I'm only sorry it wasn't me! Only joking. Hey, I'm destined for an even better relationship, I'm sure.'

Lisa sincerely hoped he was.

What was that? Lisa shot off the bed. The sound of a door closing somewhere had awakened her from a light doze. Alex must be back, she thought happily, and, smoothing the white negligé down over her slim hips, she cast a quick glance at her reflection in the mirrored wall and grinned. The astute businesswoman in the smart suit had been transformed into a sexy siren. Lisa hardly recognised herself. Alex was in for a surprise! Barefoot, she left the bedroom and padded along the hall.

'What do you wish to discuss so urgently?' The deep

velvet voice was instantly recognisable to Lisa as she approached the living room door, and sent a delicious quiver along her nerve-endings.

Then the content registered, and she swore under her breath. Damn! He had someone with him. Served her right for falling asleep, she thought ruefully. But what with getting up at the crack of dawn, working all morning, packing several suitcases, and then travelling down to London, by the time she had unpacked, showered, and had anointed her body in aromatic oil, she had lain on the bed for only five minutes before drifting off to sleep. So now what?

Well, he was her husband. She had to stop being so shy. The sitting room door was very slightly ajar and Lisa reached for its handle to push it open. But she stopped her hand in mid-air. She glanced down at herself and grimaced. She had left her long blonde hair loose, to fall in soft curls past her shoulderblades. As Alex liked it… But she doubted he would appreciate the surprise of her presence if she strolled into the living room in her diaphanous white nightgown, the lacy bodice barely covering her breasts, when he had someone with him. Then she heard the other voice and froze.

'Just a friendly chat, old boy. I thought you could give me an update on the riverside project, and a drink wouldn't go amiss.'

Unfortunately, Lisa recognised that other voice, and her heart missed a beat. The nasal tones of Nigel, her step-brother, were unmistakable.

'Scotch on the rocks?' Alex prompted, and she heard the rattle of ice on glass before Alex added. 'How did you know I was in town?'

'Simple. I rang the old man this morning, and he told me Lisa was back at work and you were spending the night in London. Can't say I blame you. Three weeks with only the ice amazon for company would have tried the patience of a saint—and you're no saint, as we all know!' A nasty chuckle completed Nigel's speech.

Lisa stiffened in anger at her stepbrother's insult, but was slightly reassured when Alex defended her.

'The lady you are referring to, happens to be my wife, and her name is Lisa. When you insult her, you insult me. You would do well to remember that.'

Lisa grinned. That's telling him, she thought, and she almost walked in on the two men at that moment. But still she hesitated. What she could not understand was how Alex knew Nigel so well. To her knowledge they had only met twice. Once at the hotel when she herself had met Alex for the first time, and again at their wedding. Yet Nigel was a visitor in Alex's penthouse, and seemingly was quite at home.

'Hey, no offence, but we're both men of the world. Which reminds me. Does the delectable Margot know you're in town for the night, alone?' Nigel's now slightly slurred tones cut into Lisa's troubled thoughts like a knife. Who was Margot?

'No, and get to the point of this visit. I must ring Lisa soon.'

'Got you on a short rein has she? Don't worry; stick her in front of a computer and she won't notice where you are. The term ''computer nerd'' was invented for the likes of Lisa. I bet she took her laptop on your honeymoon.'

Why, the insulting little toad! Lisa fumed. As it happened, she *had* brought her laptop with her this evening, to use tomorrow, but that did not make her a nerd. Nigel was only jealous because she was computer literate and he couldn't tell the difference between the Internet and a hairnet! Once more she reached out for the door, and stopped again as Alex responded.

'The only lap she was on top of was mine,' he drawled. Lisa felt the colour flood her cheeks and as quickly vanish as her new husband added, 'and that is how it is going to stay. Her working days are numbered, I can assure you.'

Deciding herself to cut back on her working life was one thing, but to have Alex arrogantly say she had to, was quite another! She loved Alex to bits, but she had no intention of letting him walk all over her. As she listened, her anger turned to horror.

'Well, that is really what I wanted to ask. I'm having a bit of a cash-flow problem, and I need your confirmation that the sale of Lawson's will go through as soon as possible. The river frontage is a goldmine, as you and I know; Shakespeare's birthplace is the ultimate tourist trap. The quicker you have the land, and I have my finder's fee and a share of the selling price, the quicker I can invest in your development plans for the site.'

Lisa leant back against the wall, her face grey beneath her golden tan, her legs trembling. She could not believe what she was hearing. Could not bear to believe it. Alex, the man she had fallen head over heels in love with, the man she had married, the man she had thought loved her, was in league with her no-good stepbrother to try and buy Lawson's and redevelop the site. She stifled the groan that rose in her throat and listened, praying it was all a mistake.

'I don't think so. I don't need any investors.' Alex's clipped tone gave her hope. Now he would denounce the whole plan. But she was wrong.

'But your man promised I could have stake in it.'

'I'll need to check, and if that is so, then of course you

can. But could you afford to? Even with your father's share of the sale? It will be *your father's share* I take it?'

'Yes. The old man doesn't need the money. He has a fat pension to look forward to. As I'm his only son and heir, it's immaterial whether he gives me the cash now or when he dies.'

'Has Harold agreed?'

'I haven't asked him yet. But he will, he never refuses me anything.'

'Lucky you. But, as I understand it, Lisa owns fifty two per cent and your father thirteen per cent; the other thirty five per cent is held by the heirs of the original partner in the firm. You're hardly going to get a fortune. In fact...' The deep, slightly accented voice dropped lower and paused tantalisingly. 'My wife is madly in love with me. She may simply give me the company without any necessity on my part to acquire the other forty-eight per cent.'

Lisa bit hard on her bottom lip to stop the cry of outrage bursting forth.

'Why you sneaky devil.' Nigel burst out.

'Enough. I would not dream of accepting a gift of that size from a lady, not even my wife. I don't believe in being beholden to anyone, man or woman,'

'Sorry. No, of course not. But are you sure Lisa will go along with your plan for Lawson's? Her mother flatly refused to sell a year ago.'

'A year ago Lisa had not met me. Now she is my wife, and soon, hopefully, the mother of my children. I can safely say she will not have the time or the inclination to continue at work. She will do as I say. You have nothing to worry about Nigel. You will get yours; I promise you that.'

Lisa closed her eyes, her whole body shivering with

pain and anger. The shocking discovery that her husband was about to betray her, not with another woman but with her stepbrother, had cut to the very centre of her being. It had razored her nerves and turned her into a seething mass of conflicting emotions.

Alex's love, the wedding, *everything* had been one big sham. Alex and Nigel were plotting between them to take over Lawson's. To redevelop the site! Over her dead body, Lisa vowed.

The week her mother had been diagnosed as having cancer, an approach had been made to buy Lawson's. Lisa racked her brains but she could not remember the name of the company. It certainly had not been Solomos International and there had been no mention of redeveloping the site; developing a partnership had been the impression given. Her mother, Harold and herself had briefly discussed it at the time. Her mother had decided against it; Lawson's Designer Glass was to stay a family firm as a memorial to Peter, and, as it happened a few months later, also to herself.

Lisa shuddered. The pain was waiting for her, she knew, but with brutal determination she blocked it out and allowed rage, fierce and primeval, to consume her mind. For a second she was tempted to burst into the living room and confront the two rats who were plotting against her...

Instead, ice-cold reasoning prevailed. She did not need to hear any more, and silently she returned to the master bedroom.

CHAPTER TWO

LISA started towards the dressing room, her first thought to get dressed and go. Then she realised the futility of such a gesture. In order to leave she would have to confront Alex, and she was not ready to do that. She doubted she ever would be.

She shivered anew, not with pain but remembered pleasure. Alex, her husband, her lover! He only had to look at her and she went weak at the knees. She and a few million other women, she tried to tell herself. And how many of the other, faceless women had known the wonder of his lovemaking, the seductive power of his caress, his kiss, the magnificent strength of his sleek, hard, toned body?

Lisa groaned in disgust at her own weak will and, swinging around, glanced at the bed. Very soon now, Alex would ring the house at Stratford-upon-Avon and discover from Harold that she had left to join him in London. Panicking, she crossed to the large patio window that opened out on to the balcony and slid it open. Stepping out, she took a few deep breaths in an effort to calm down. Tomorrow was Mid-summer's Day and tonight was clear and light, although it was ten o'clock. A panoramic view of London stretched out before her, tinged with gold as the evening sun slid towards the distant horizon. Much the same as her confidence in her marriage was sliding into oblivion, she thought bitterly.

She squared her shoulders; self-pity was an emotion she despised. She had to think, to do something, but what? It was still warm; she could spend the night outside. Fool! Alex was bound to look for her.

Slowly she turned and reluctantly entered the bedroom again; her eyes slid back to the huge bed, the imprint of where she had catnapped on the coverlet clearly visible. Her head jerked up at the sound of a door closing. Nigel departing, maybe? Any minute now, Alex would make the phone call and discover her whereabouts. Lisa did the only thing she could. She lay back down on the bed. Perhaps if she pretended to be asleep Alex would not wake her. She prayed he would be fooled, because, if not, she had no confidence in her ability to resist the magnetic pull of his virile sensuality. Even knowing Alex had only married her for a business deal, knowing what a wicked, callous swine he was, was still no protection against the force of his potent personality.

Closing her eyes, Lisa feigned sleep, but her mind spun with images of the past. It had seemed so simple not two months ago, when she had fallen in love with Alex at first sight. Fate, Kismet...

It had been Harold's birthday and Nigel had arrived at their Stratford-upon-Avon home unannounced. He had insisted his father and Lisa had mourned long enough for her mother and that he was taking them both out for a meal at the top hotel in the area.

With hindsight Lisa realised she should have guessed there was something funny going on, because experience had taught her that Nigel only ever visited his father if he wanted something, usually money. His appearance in Statford-upon-Avon on his father's birthday had been the first time she had seen him since her mother's funeral. For Harold's sake, she had agreed to the dinner date, and at nine in the evening the three of them had been sitting in the hotel's cocktail bar, enjoying after-dinner coffee and Cognacs, when Alex had strolled into the bar.

Lisa would never forget the moment when she had looked up and seen Alex Solomos for the first time. Her body had reacted as if in shock. She'd forgotten to breathe! He was an attractive man, but it had been more than that. Something about him had called out to her innermost being; her stomach had churned and her heart had raced out of control. She'd felt as if she had been struck by lightning.

Wearing a black dinner suit and a brilliant white dress shirt—a perfect foil for his olive-skinned complexion— and standing head and shoulders above every other male in the room, he'd crossed to the bar in a few lithe strides. She'd watched as he'd ordered a drink, before turning around and resting his superbly muscled long-limbed body against the bar. His dark gaze had casually scanned the room his eyes bored.

Lisa, wide eyed and wondrous, had found she could do nothing but stare. Then she'd blushed to the roots of her hair when his deep-set eyes had met hers, and then travelled on down over her body, widening in obvious appreciation on the length of her long legs. She'd been wearing a short black sheath dress and reclining on a low sofa, inadvertently exposing rather more leg than she'd realised. His head had lifted, making eye contact again, before swerving to take in her two male companions. A cynical dismissive smile had twisted his firm lips, and he'd continued his perusal of the room.

Gorgeous, but arrogant with it, Lisa had thought, and, nervously tugging at the hem of her dress, she'd forced herself to look away, taking a swift swallow of her coffee to hide her scarlet face. She had experienced sexual chemistry before, but this was ridiculous.

'Well, I'll be damned.' Nigel had said softly. 'The great man himself, Alex Solomos.' Turning to Lisa, he had added. 'Do you know who he is?'

'I haven't the slightest idea,' she replied coolly, fighting down an urge to ask Nigel to tell her all about the stranger. Along with the urge to mentally strip the man naked!

'You must have heard of Leo Solomos, his father?'

'No, should I have done?' she queried.

Nigel's pale eyes narrowed rather warily on her face. 'Probably not, unless you read the gossip pages in the gutter press. Leo Solomos is a Greek tycoon. But he's rather better known for the number of ladies he has married. The man at the bar is his son. He keeps a much lower profile, but it's well known in financial circles that he's the power behind the throne. The old man would have gone bust years ago, simply because of alimony payments, if it wasn't for Alex Solomos taking control of the company.'

Lisa sneaked a furtive glance back at the man from beneath the mask of her long lashes; she could well believe Nigel. Alex Solomos, with his impressive height and magnificent build, looked every inch the dynamic, powerful businessman.

'Wait here you two, I'm going to introduce myself. This is too good an opportunity to miss.' And, to Lisa's horror, her stepbrother approached the man at the bar, and started to talk.

'Harold, does Nigel know that man?' she asked after a few minutes, only too well aware of her stepbrother's penchant for pushing in where he was not wanted.

'Well, he does now, Lisa.' Harold quipped, with a nod in the direction of the bar.

Lisa looked up, and her stomach lurched. Nigel was returning, with the stunning man in tow. Helplessly, she stared at his face. He was incredibly attractive, with classically sculptured features, a mobile, sensual mouth that was twitching in the beginnings of a smile.

'Nigel suggested I join you for a drink. I hope you don't mind?' He turned all the force of his megawatt smile on Lisa, no trace of his earlier cynicism present.

'You are a friend of his?' she managed to ask, trying not to stare, and wondering how such a superior example of the male species could possibly like Nigel.

'Not really. Apparently he recognised me and took pity on a man drinking alone. But seemingly we do have a mutual business acquaintance.' His voice was low and a little husky, with just the slightest trace of an accent. 'Allow me to introduce myself. Alex Solomos.'

The hand he held out to Lisa was large and tanned, and when his fingers curled around hers, the heat and strength he generated seemed to sizzle right through her whole body. Lisa looked up into a pair of heavy lidded dark brown eyes, and the intensity of his gaze held her mesmerised.

'Lisa—Lisa Lawson,' she stammered, and she did not breathe again until he let go of her hand.

Turning to shake Harold's hand, he said, 'And you are Nigel's father, I believe. There is no mistaking the likeness.'

The three men talked and ordered another round of drinks while Lisa tried hard not to stare at Alex. She was a businesswoman, not some lovestruck teenager, but it was no good. A heady excitement made her blood fizz like champagne in her veins. His hard handsome face, his eyes, drew her gaze like a magnet, and his voice sounded like a caress to her over-sensitive nerves.

Apparently he was in Stratford for the weekend. He had been to see a performance of *Richard III*.

'I confess I left at the first interval. My English is good, but not so good I can understand the language of Shakespeare.'

Somehow his confession that he had walked out on the play rather than pretend he understood it endeared him to Lisa even more, and from that moment on she was a goner...

Alex left half an hour later for a dinner engagement, and Lisa found herself giving him her address. He arranged to pick her up at ten the next morning, in the pretence that she would act as his guide around Stratford for the day.

When he called for her the next morning, casually dressed in blue denim jeans and a black cashmere sweater, she had simply stared.

'You're even more beautiful than I remembered.' His brown eyes darkened with an unmistakable message in their depths, leaving her more flustered than she had ever been in her life. He helped her into the passenger seat of a lethal-looking red sports car and then slid into the driver's seat. But before starting the car, he turned to her with dark, serious eyes.

'There is something I have to tell you, Lisa.' For one heart-chilling moment she thought he was going to tell her he was married. 'I am the boss of Solomos International. Is that going to be a problem for you?'

The relief was so great, Lisa beamed. She was a confident, intelligent young woman, she dressed in designer clothes or snappy casuals, and she could mix in any strata of society. She never gave it much thought, but actually, on paper, she was also wealthy. He had no need to worry; she wouldn't be intimidated by his money. It was in the sexual stakes she was a novice, nowhere else. 'No, of course not. I am the boss of Lawson's, but I never mix business with pleasure,' she said, daringly for her. And she was rewarded by a reciprocal brilliant smile.

'Good. Beautiful and sensible. A winning combination.'

It was the best day of Lisa's life. They walked hand in hand by the river and around the streets of Stratford-upon-Avon and talked about everything and nothing. He insisted on driving out of town for lunch. They shared a ploughman's lunch in the garden of a small country pub, Alex teasingly feeding her a small cherry tomato with his fingers. As Lisa opened her mouth his glance fixed on her face, his eyes dark and hot, and when his fingers touched her lips, she felt a surge of desire so strong she trembled and could not hide it from him.

'It is the same for me, Lisa,' he had told her in a deep, husky voice, and when she blushed, he added with a tender smile, 'The sexual chemistry between us is electric, but have no fear, Lisa, I will not take advantage of you; it's not my style.'

For the rest of the day they enjoyed themselves like a couple of children. By Sunday evening, she was so captivated by him that when he took her into his arms and kissed her, and told her he was going to marry her, her answer was a joyous yes. The following weekend he stayed at her home in Stratford, and formally asked Harold for her hand in marriage. Three weeks later they were married.

Thinking about it now, Lisa cringed in shame at her own naivety. She should have guessed Nigel had had a hidden agenda when he'd introduced her to Alex. But she'd had little experience of men. As a teenager she'd been taller than most of the girls at her school, and had been tormented about being gawky. So when other girls had been dating, Lisa had concentrated on her studies.

Later, she had never seemed to have the time for soci-
alising. In fact her best friend, if she was honest, was Jed,
whom she'd never met in person.

'Lisa, Lisa, darling.' Lost in her own troubled thoughts,
she hadn't been conscious of Alex entering the room. She
heard his deep voice and closed her eyes. How she was
going to get through the night, she had no idea, and for
a fleeting instant she wished she could turn the clock back
to this morning. If she had stayed in Stratford, she would
have been perfectly happy, but by coming to London she
had discovered more than she'd ever wanted to know.

'Lisa.' Alex's deep, husky drawl feathered across her
cheek. She felt the mattress depress and knew she had no
chance of pretending to sleep.

'Alex,' she murmured, turning over on to her back and
blinking her bright blue eyes, as though she had just
woken up.

'This is a surprise.' He gave her a narrow-eyed look.
'Unexpected, but very flattering. When did you arrive?'

Was it her imagination or was there more to the seemingly innocuous question? Did he suspect she might have
overheard his conversation with Nigel?

'What time is it?' She answered his question with one
of her own. Her stomach was churning with a mixture of
distress and desire.

'Ten-thirty.'

'Oh, I got here at eight, bathed and changed, and I must
have fallen asleep an hour or so ago.' She tried to smile,
badly shaken by his close proximity and the proprietorial
hand he curved around her naked shoulder.

Slowly his lips parted over brilliant white teeth, in a
broad smile with just a tinge of smugness. 'Couldn't stay
away from me, hmm?' His gaze lingered on her mouth.

'Something like that,' Lisa whispered, when in reality

she felt like lifting her hand and decking him! She felt furious, and sickened at having been taken in by him so easily. His head lowered and his mouth moved closer and it took all her will-power not to take a bite out of the sensuous lips that closed over hers.

'I need a shower. Come and join me,' Alex husked some moments later.

'What, and waste all the obscenely expensive body oil I have applied for your benefit?' she tried to tease.

'There is something very satisfying about a woman who will go to so much trouble for her man,' Alex drawled, his dark eyes gleaming with an equally teasing light. 'Give me five minutes to shower, and then I am at your mercy. I expect to be thoroughly seduced.'

'Of course. Why else would I be here?' Watching the arrogant set of his broad shoulders as he walked across to the bathroom, she wished she had the courage to tell him to go to hell. Far from seducing him, she felt like strangling him. She was wild with anger, but deep down she knew his lightest touch could send her senses reeling, and his kiss made her ache for more.

As soon as she heard the shower running, Lisa leapt off the bed. No way was she going to be lying there waiting for him like some harem slave! Restlessly she crossed to the patio window and gazed blindly out. How had she got herself in such a mess? She had been fooled by Alex's sophistication, his stunning good looks and the kind of blatant sexuality that had set up an answering need in her own untried body. It hurt so much to discover Alex had not been honest with her. She had given him her trust, completely and unconditionally, and all the time he'd been in league with Nigel.

In one way she thought it might have hurt less if there had been another woman. At least Alex could have claimed to be overtaken by passion. But to have married her in cold blood to pursue a business deal showed a degree of ruthlessness, a contempt for her as a person that she could not come to terms with.

'I'm all yours, darling.' Alex's deep voice broke into her musings and turning around, she gave a strangled gasp. He was totally naked and completely unconcerned as he strode across the room and lay down on the bed, and patted the space beside him. 'Don't keep me waiting, or I might just fall asleep. I've had a hell of a day. But the night is certainly looking better.' He grinned. 'Be gentle with me, won't you?'

It was the grin that did it... Her blue eyes flashed to his, and she saw the gleam of amusement in the deep, dark depths of his brown eyes, along with a glitter of sexual anticipation. The bastard! she thought. I'll show him. Crossing to the bed, she stripped her nightgown over her head and standing proud and naked, she asked, 'Where would you like me to start first darling, top or bottom?'

Without waiting for his answer she draped herself over him, catching his head between her hands. Her mouth fastened on his and she kissed him with all the rage and passion of a woman cheated by love. *Heav'n has no rage, like love to hate turn'd, Nor Hell a fury, like a woman scorn'd.* The quotation leapt into Lisa's mind, and in that moment she knew it was true.

She did not want his tenderness; it was false anyway. Deliberately she nipped his full lower lip between her white teeth, and then dropped lower to bite at his strong neck. She was like a woman possessed in her rage, and Alex's deep, throaty chuckle only incensed her further. She felt his arm close around her waist. His other hand slid between their two bodies to capture one full breast, and rolled her aching nipple between his finger and thumb. She groaned out loud and retaliated by tonguing on his male nipple in a passion of her own, straddling him with her long legs trapping his. She felt his burgeoning arousal and delighted in it.

'So you want to play rough, my lovely Lisa?' Alex husked.

She lifted her head and her blue eyes blazed down into his eyes, which were dark with sexual need. 'You have no idea how rough,' she whispered, the breath exiting her body in a rush as he raised his head and sucked one of her taut nipples into his mouth. Lisa raked his chest with her nails and strained back. Alex laughed, and twisted his hand in her long hair, his lips meeting hers, his tongue delving deep into the hot, moist depths of her mouth while he moved his body against hers. His other arm wrapped around her like a steel band.

Lisa wriggled against him. She was so hot, so furious, and perspiration beaded her skin, but even in her anger, when Alex swung her beneath him, she opened her mouth to give a helpless moan. In a tangle of arms and legs they rolled around the bed, Lisa determined to be the dominant one, but Alex not about to let her.

They battled for supremacy as they kissed, bit and caressed in a storm of unbridled passion, each seeing who could give the other the most pleasure, and finally they came together in a wild, hungry mating that took them both to the heights of ecstasy. Lisa cried out at the intensity of it, and her cries mingled with Alex's as his body shuddered in spasm after spasm of prolonged pleasure.

Afterwards, when Alex lay by her side in total exhaustion, Lisa knew this had been the best ever, and also the worst. The worst because it had revealed her deepest fear:

she could not resist Alex; even in her rage and anger she felt love.

Alex stirred, and, putting a possessive arm around her shoulder, he said, 'If I didn't know I am your only lover, I might be suspicious of your new-found aggressive sexuality.' And with the pounding of his heart almost back to normal, he added, 'But I knew the moment I saw you that you had a deeply sensuous nature and it only needed the right man to reveal it.'

Lisa glanced sideways at him. 'And you're the right man?' She'd meant to sound sarcastic but instead the breathless tone of her voice sounded as if she agreed with him. Filled with shame at her own behaviour, she quickly looked away.

Alex chuckled. 'Of course.' Tucking her firmly under his arm, he yawned widely. 'Remind me to leave you alone more often, if tonight's episode is to be the result, hmm?' He yawned again.

She stared at him. He looked like some great slumbering lion lying on the bed, his eyes half closed, his broad chest rising and falling in rhythm to the deep beat of his heart, his mouth curved in a satisfied smile, content and assured of his masculine virility.

In that moment Lisa did not know whether she wanted to hit him, or hug him. Instead, to her horror, she heard herself ask the one question that had tormented her for the past few hours. 'Do you really love me, Alex?'

'After what we have just done, need you ask?' he murmured, already half asleep.

But sleep did not come so easily for Lisa. She was tormented by the thought that Alex and Nigel were plotting together. But, seduced by the warmth of his body and the protective arm around her shoulder, slowly Lisa felt her anger began to drain away. Maybe she had been too hasty in her conclusion. It was perfectly possible her first meeting with Alex had been a set-up, but that did not necessarily mean that what had happened next had been a lie.

Lisa turned on her side and examined her sleeping husband. In repose he looked younger than his thirty-five years, his black hair tumbling in disarray across his broad forehead. She reached out and brushed the offending lock of hair back, but Alex did not stir. Sleeping the sleep of the innocent. But was he?

Sighing, Lisa turned on to her back and gazed at the ceiling. Perhaps she had overreacted. She loved Alex, and up until tonight she had been sure he loved her. He hadn't been able to wait to marry her. Thinking about it now, Lisa decided his haste to marry her could not have been solely for business reasons. He could easily have waited a few more weeks, so it had to have been because he had wanted her. In fact, she probably had nothing to worry about. The solution was in her own hands. If, or when, she was approached to sell her company and asked to agree to flatten it—which was worse—she would simply refuse. If Alex made any comment then, and only then, would she discover the absolute truth.

Her decision made, she closed her eyes and tried to sleep. If she was being honest with herself, she knew she was taking a coward's way out by deciding to wait, rather than confront Alex with what she had overheard straight away. But she was giving herself time. Time to share his life and his love. If tonight had taught her anything at all, it was that she was hopelessly in love with him and could not resist him even when she thought she hated him.

Oh, my God! Suddenly Lisa was wide awake, because she had overlooked one very important fact. From the conversation she had overheard, Alex did not know yet that she had donated five per cent of her shares in Lawson Designer Glass to the hospice! It had never entered Lisa's head that the charity, at some future date, might sell the shares. But with a ruthless operator like Alex on the prowl she had to see it as a possibility.

If the hospice and the Lee estate sold to Alex, that would leave Harold with the deciding vote in the company. Much as she loved her stepfather, she hadn't a lot of faith in his ability to resist the demands of his son. Nigel was his one blind spot. As she actually owned only forty seven percent of the company, she would lose overall control! How could she have been so stupid?

Finally, with a brief glance at her sleeping husband, she slipped out of bed. A hot drink might cure her insomnia. Pulling on Alex's discarded shirt, she buttoned it up and padded barefoot from the bedroom, along the hall and into the living area. It was a huge room, with a raised dining area, and seating at its opposite end arranged to take full advantage of the view through a wall of glass, with doors that opened out on to a roof garden. Architecturally, it was a magnificent room, but the plain black leather seating, the clean lines of the elm wood furniture and the polished hardwood floor had an oddly sterile look in the bright silver light of the moon. There was nothing personal or homely about it; in fact it looked exactly what it was: a company penthouse.

Lisa walked the length of the room to where double doors opened into a wide hall. At one side of it was the door leading to the kitchen and on the other side another two doors, one of the cloakroom and the other of Alex's study. At the end of the hallway stood a half screen in marble and glass and, beyond that the actual entrance door to the apartment.

Lisa entered the kitchen and switched on the light,

pushing the door almost shut behind her. In a matter of minutes she'd made a cup of hot chocolate and, sitting down at the breakfast table, she cupped the mug in her hands and sipped it slowly, her brain spinning with confusion. Alex and Nigel! If she hadn't heard them with her own ears, she would never have believed it, and yet it seemed they were planning on being business partners, at the expense of *her* business! The mind boggled...

If she felt more secure in her marriage, the sensible thing to do would be to confront Alex and demand an explanation. But it was too late now; she could hardly admit it tomorrow without looking a fool. No, her earlier decision was the best. Wait and see, and hopefully Alex would prove her wrong.

Suddenly an odd noise made Lisa straighten up in her chair. It sounded like a key turning in a lock.

Hardly daring to breathe, Lisa very quietly put the mug down on the table, her back stiffening with tension. Someone had let himself into the apartment. She heard footsteps on the polished wood of the entrance foyer floor. It had to be a burglar! She thought of screaming for Alex, but he was sound asleep at the other end of the apartment.

Glancing frantically around the kitchen, Lisa looked for something with which to defend herself from the intruder. A shelf of bright orange pans caught her eye. They were a well-known French make, and heavy. Silently she got to her feet and, picking up the largest saucepan from the shelf with the utmost stealth crossed to the slightly open kitchen door.

A very feminine giggle stopped Lisa in her tracks. Her blue eyes widened in amazement. A red-headed woman was bent over, and rather unsteadily removing a pair of high-heeled shoes at the entrance to the living room. As Lisa watched the woman straightened, her red lace stole falling to the floor behind her to reveal a strapless, back-less, red sheath dress. Then she spoke, before walking into the living room. 'Alex, darling. Sorry I'm late, and you're all on your ownsome.'

This was no burglar, Lisa thought bitterly, and for a long moment shock held her rigid. The woman had a key for the apartment; the woman knew Alex was alone to-night, or was supposed to be. No! her heart screamed. The colour drained from her face. Was it only a few hours ago when she had thought Alex's betrayal with her stepbrother was the worst that could happen to her? Her soft mouth twisted with savage irony. She had even thought then that it would be less painful if Alex had been overcome with passion for another woman. She had been wrong...

She dared not move, convinced she would splinter like glass into a million pieces, feeling as if each shard would pierce straight in her heart. How long she stood there she had no idea.

Finally Lisa became aware of the saucepan in her hand, and automatically crossed the floor to put it back where she had found it. Then, zombie-like, she left the kitchen and followed the woman as she saw her disappearing into the corridor that housed the four bedrooms.

She was in time to see the woman enter the bedroom Lisa herself had only recently vacated. The door was wide open and bright moonlight flooded the scene. The other woman was totally unaware of Lisa, all her attention fixed on Alex, lying sprawled across the bed, the sheet covering the essentials and nothing much else of him. As Lisa watched in horrified fascination, the woman stepped out of her dress. She was not wearing a bra, only a pair of thong briefs, and as one small hand reached out to lift the sheet, at the same time one elegant leg was raised.

Lisa could take no more. The frozen horror that had

held her immobile snapped, and she was toweringly, furiously mad. She switched on the central light.

Three things happened at once. The woman in the act of climbing into bed fell back, as Alex opened his eyes and shot bolt upright in bed. 'Margot? What the hell—'

Lisa's face was white, a frozen mask of rage, and the glance she threw at Alex should have burned him to a crisp. But with a glance at the woman leaning against the bed, he returned her look with one of puzzled fury.

'How did she get in here?' he demanded of Lisa.

They said attack was the best line of defence, and obviously that was Alex's strategy, Lisa thought contemptuously. 'The lady has a key. You appear to hand them out like candy bars at Hallowe'en. But don't let me interrupt. I'll just get my things and go.'

Marching into the room, she headed for the dressing room, but Alex stopped her. He had leapt out of bed stark naked, and now grabbed her by the shoulders.

'Don't be ridiculous, Lisa, this is all a terrible mistake. Surely you can see that?'

'I can see everything,' she snorted with a derisive scan of his body, 'and so can your lady-friend. But then there's nothing she hasn't seen before.'

Suddenly made aware of his naked state, between the avid eyes of the woman standing by the bed and the icy cold eyes of his wife, Alex let fly with a string of what could only be curses in Greek, while grabbing the sheet from the bed and wrapping it around himself. Free of his hold, Lisa headed for the door.

'Not so fast,' he growled, and caught her arm. 'You must have seen Margot come in here. Why didn't you stop her? You're my *wife* for heaven's sake.'

Lisa could not believe the audacity of the man. His girlfriend had walked into his apartment, stripped almost

naked and had been about to slip into his bed. Yet somehow Alex was making it *her* fault! Not one word of cen-
sure to the girlfriend!

'Was,' she said trenchantly, and tried to shrug off his
restraining hand. When pulling free didn't work Lisa
changed tactics and elbowed him violently in his stomach.
It had the desired result as the air whooshed out of him
and he let go of her arm. But only for a second. She had
barely time to turn round before he had caught her by the
wrist again.

'Enough, Lisa,' he growled, spinning her around to face
him. Lisa stared at him. He was seethingly angry; she
could sense it in the tautness of his features and the cold
black depths of his eyes. 'Where the hell do you think
you're going?'

'You know the saying—two's company, three's a
crowd,' she shot back furiously. 'I'm leaving.'

He shook her arm, his mouth a tight, menacing line.
'You are not going anywhere.' His black eyes held Lisa's
in a fierce challenge, daring her to disagree.

'Oops, I seem to have made a mistake.' Margot's voice
cut through the electric tension in the air.

Both Lisa and Alex turned to look at the woman with
equal degrees of anger.

'Sorry, I must have got the day wrong. I could have
sworn it was tonight.'

Lisa took a really good look at the other woman. She
had small breasts and a tiny waist, but she was not a
natural redhead. On seeing the woman's face for the first
time, Lisa's eyes widened in stunned recognition. Her picture had been on posters around Stratford-upon-Avon a
couple of months ago. It was Margot Delfont, an up-and-
coming Shakespearean actress.

'Margot, get dressed and get out,' Alex commanded. 'I've told you it's over.'

'But after two years I didn't think you meant it, Alex, darling.' Margot replied lightly, though Lisa saw the naked pleading in the other woman's eyes and had to look away. 'I mean, that was weeks ago, and we've had tiffs before, and got over them.'

'How many weeks ago? Seven?' Lisa asked, but she already knew the answer.

'Not now, Lisa,' Alex snapped at her. Then, picking the red dress off the floor, he walked across to Margot and threw it at her. 'Out.'

But Lisa saw it all now. The first time she had met Alex he had said he was in Stratford for the theatre, but had left early. He hadn't been there for the play but obviously to see his girlfriend. Lisa's lips twisted in the travesty of a smile. Alex had had a drink with Harold, Nigel and herself, before pleading a late dinner engagement and leaving, but only after having made quite sure he could see Lisa the next day. The phrase 'killing two birds with one stone' sprang to mind...

A night with his lover and a bid for the property Lisa owned. What a naive fool she had been! Lisa clenched her teeth to stop herself crying out in pain.

'Look, I'm awfully sorry, darling, but really it is no big deal. In fact, it might be rather fun with a threesome,' Margot suggested, smiling up at Alex as she shimmied into her dress. And then, turning her attention to Lisa, she added, 'I'm sorry, we haven't been introduced, but you must be the new wife. So what do you say?'

Lisa shook her head in complete disgust. It was like a black comedy, and she would not demean herself with a response.

'Margot, shut up and get out.' Not by a flicker of an

eyelash did Alex betray his feelings. He simply gave the woman standing by the bed a cold, impersonal inspection. 'And leave the key behind this time.'

Lisa didn't know which one she hated more. Margot, or her arrogant husband. She almost felt sorry for Margot; it was obvious she loved Alex, and would do anything, anything at all for him! But it was equally obvious he cared little or nothing for her; she had been a convenient body in his bed when he had needed a woman.

Alex turned back to Lisa, sliding a proprietoral arm around her waist. 'This is all an unfortunate mistake.'

Lisa glanced up at him. A mistake, he'd said, but it was Lisa who had made one. Alex didn't feel any more for her than he did for Margot. His handsome face was expressionless; he was not at all embarrassed by the ludicrous situation he found himself in. Because he didn't really care for either woman...

The realisation galvanised Lisa into action. With an almighty jerk and a hefty kick to Alex's shin, she broke away, and was out of the door and straight into the guest room across the hall, slamming the door behind her. Luckily it had a lock, and swiftly she turned the key. She flung back her head and took deep, shaky breaths, trying to force the air into her lungs. She saw the light switch and pressed it on. The sudden glare hurt her eyes and she doubled over. Her stomach churned and she knew she was going to be sick. Stumbling into the adjoining bathroom, she bent over the toilet bowl.

CHAPTER THREE

How had she never realised what kind of man she was marrying? Lisa asked herself over and over again. She tore off the shirt she was wearing, she didn't want anything of Alex's near her. Then she crossed to the washbasin and splashed her face with cold water and cleaned her teeth, trying to take the taste of nausea from her mouth. She filled a glass with water and drank it. She was shivering, more with shock than cold, and, glancing around the bathroom, she saw a robe provided for guests on top of a pile of fresh towels by the bath.

Picking up the thick white towelling robe, she slipped it on, tying the belt firmly around her waist. Yet still she was shaking. She had half expected Alex to follow her. She walked into the bedroom and glanced around; it was pleasant, if a bit like a hotel room. A double bed in the centre of one wall. At one side a soft-cushioned sofa and an occasional table, a cabinet that housed a television, video and CD players. Against the wall to the left of the door was a desk and office centre. The three guest bedrooms of the apartment, Lisa knew, were all equipped in the same fashion. Alex had told her this was his base in the UK, so it also doubled as a company apartment. The master suite and his study remained locked when he was not in residence, but the place was occasionally used by visiting executives and for corporate entertainment. A bitter smile twisted her soft lips. Alex had failed to add he also used it for strictly personal, sexual entertainment.

In the distance she heard a door slam. Had the luscious

Margot left? She didn't know and she no longer cared, she told herself. She had no illusions left. She had made a horrendous mistake, marrying a man she hardly knew, but she would get over it—she had to. She closed her eyes for a second and immediately saw in her mind's eye the face of Margot, and the expression in the woman's eyes came back to haunt her. Margot had looked at Alex with slavish, sick desire, and how had Alex reacted? By ordering her out. Yet, for two years, if Margot was to be believed, he had used the woman quite shamelessly.

Lisa opened her eyes, and in that moment she vowed she would never become so enslaved to any man again, especially not her husband. Alex had betrayed her trust, and it hurt. *How it hurt.* But he would never get the chance to do it again… She raised her hands and swept the tangled mass of her hair back from her face and straightened her shoulders. The shivering had stopped and she began to think logically about the night's events.

Dear heaven! She shook her head, appalled at her own stupidity. She could see clearly now. Alex, Margot and Nigel were all alike: immoral, money-hungry, selfish. What sort of fool did they take her for? The only way Margot could have known Alex was going to be alone tonight was if Alex had told her. A harsh laugh escaped her. Her over-sexed husband had made one mistake. In his hurry to let Lisa seduce him he had forgotten to ring his girlfriend and tell her their date was off. Thinking about it now, Lisa supposed she should be flattered his desire for her had overcome his usual controlled efficient self. But she wasn't.

'Lisa, open the door.' Alex's deep voice broke the silence of the night. She saw the handle turn and then he knocked. 'Open the door, Lisa, we have to talk.'

Not in this lifetime, she thought bitterly. She had nothing to say to him.

The banging got louder.

'Please, Lisa, open the door. I really need to talk to you.' The husky, sensual tone of his voice enraged Lisa; it was all an act.

'Get lost,' she yelled back.

'Open the damned door Lisa.' The doorhandle rattled ferociously.

'No.'

'I will count to three and then I will break the thing down,' Alex declared.

It was too much to hope that he would leave her alone. Wiping her damp palms down the soft towelling covering her thighs, she reluctantly turned the key in the lock. She had to jump back as the door swung in and Alex burst into the room.

'Lisa!' His hands grabbed her shoulders and he pulled her towards him. 'What do you think you're playing at, locking me out?' His eyes flared angrily; his fingers gripped her shoulders.

She planted her hands on his chest and shoved hard. 'Let go of me,' she cried, and lifted her knee, her intention plain. He jerked back, but did not release her.

'Lisa, Lisa, calm down and let me explain.' He tried to appease her, but she was having none of it.

'There is nothing to explain. I saw it all. And as for calming down,' she said angrily, her blue eyes like chips of ice, 'I'll calm down when you get out of my sight.'

'You don't mean that,' he growled, pulling her hard against him once more. His mouth swooped on hers with savage anger. She twisted her head—anything to avoid his kiss. But one hand tangled in her hair, as his arm curved around her waist, clamping her firmly to his long body. She tried to wriggle free as he took her mouth with a ruthless passion that would not be denied.

But, even as she felt insidious warmth building inside her she recognised his strategy and was sickened by it. He was blatantly using his sexual prowess to overcome her. Her eyes clashed with his and she saw the implacable intent in their black depths, and she froze in his arms.

'No,' she said flatly, and at her withdrawal Alex lifted his head; what he saw in her face, gave him pause.

'Your response was a bit lacking in enthusiasm. Does this mean the honeymoon is over?' he queried cynically.

'Not just the honeymoon. The marriage as well.' She ignored the burning pain around her heart. Alex had only been able to deceive her so easily because she had wanted to believe in the myth of love at first sight. She felt him tense, and as his hands fell away from her she was free.

'Now you're being ridiculous, Lisa.' he told her curtly. 'The little scene with Margot was embarrassing for all concerned, but there is no reason to be so melodramatic. We will probably laugh about it later.'

She looked at him in the harsh glare of the overhead light. He was standing a foot away. His tall body was covered in a burgundy velvet robe, with satin lapels that fell open to reveal his curling chest hair. The belt was tied firmly around his waist but the garment ended a few inches above his knee, exposing a long length of strong tanned leg.

'You might. I won't,' she bit out, refusing to be intimidated by his towering presence. 'Somehow, finding a woman crawling into my husband's bed not fifteen minutes after I vacated it does not strike me as a cause for amusement.' Turning her back on him, she walked across the room towards the sofa. She couldn't bear to look at him.

'Wait just a minute.' A strong hand wrapped around her arm and stopped her in her tracks. She glanced up at him. He looked dark and dangerous and for a second a shiver of apprehension slithered down her spine. 'Don't you think you're overreacting? It was hardly my fault the woman called here.'

'Hardly your fault?' Lisa almost choked at the gall of the man. She was bitterly angry, angrier than she had been when she had overheard his conversation with Nigel. To be betrayed once was bad enough, but twice in one night! 'Oh, please! Spare me the excuses.'

Alex was silent for a long moment, watching her with narrowed eyes. 'I do not make excuses to anyone.' She saw his face harden 'And certainly not to my wife who, only a few short hours ago, could not keep her hands off me.'

Trust him to remind her. 'But then I didn't expect a few hours later to see another woman crawling into your bed,' she returned with icy sarcasm.

'If you had stayed in our bed, it would never have happened. I'd like an explanation.'

'You want an explanation? That's rich,' Lisa said hotly, backing away a few paces, but Alex followed, until her back came into contact with the wall. 'Especially coming from a man like you.'

'So, humour me, wife,' he drawled tightly, his eyes burning on her. 'Because I have had just about enough for one night.'

She debated telling him to drop dead, but quickly dismissed the notion. He was standing looking down on her, his hands placed on the wall behind her, his body effectively trapping her. His black eyes leapt with anger, and she realised he was in a towering rage. Probably at being caught out, but she had no intention of testing him. She

was hanging on to her sanity by a thread. She simply
wanted him to leave her alone.

'I got up to make a cup of hot chocolate. I was in the
kitchen; I heard the sound of the door, and thought it was
a burglar. I picked up a pan to challenge the intruder with,
and crept to the hall door.' Her eyes flashed with renewed
rage as she added, 'But lo and behold, it was a lady.'

'Why didn't you yell for me, or stop her?' Alex demanded. 'Surely those were the obvious things to do.'

'Because I heard her speak.' And in an exaggerated
voice Lisa continued, *"Alex, darling. Sorry I'm so late,
and you're all on your ownsome."* Her eyes hated him
as she rashly held his gaze. 'The lady could not have
known you were going to be alone tonight unless you'd
told her. My surprise arrival really upset your plan, didn't
it?' She snorted her disgust. 'Now get out of my way.'

'For a girl who avowed her undying love not a month
ago, you certainly have a fine opinion of me,' Alex
drawled sardonically. 'Do you really think I asked Margot
to come here?'

'Who else?' She raised one perfectly arched brow in
query.

'I don't usually explain my actions to anyone, but in
this case I will make an exception.' She looked at him,
and for the briefest of moments he looked away as he
hesitated. Lisa did not need to hear any more. She knew
him for the liar he was.

'It doesn't matter.' Bone weary and sick at heart, she
had neither the will nor the energy to fight with him.

'But it does.' He lifted his hand and cupped her chin
before she could turn away, his breath warm against her
skin, his dark eyes holding hers in fierce purpose. 'Margot
was at a nightclub and spoke to a man I'd had a meeting
with today. I had mentioned I was staying in town tonight

and that he could call me here with some information I required. Obviously in the course of his conversation with Margot he must have let slip the fact. As for her having the key to the apartment—it is true we did have an affair, but I broke it off before I met you.'

'Your poor girlfriend didn't seem to think so,' Lisa said scathingly.

'Don't waste your pity on Margot; she was under no illusion about our relationship. It was never going anywhere; it simply mutually benefited both parties.'

'If you say so,' she responded grimly. 'But, actually, I don't really care.' And at that moment she didn't; she had taken too many shocks for one night, and simply wanted to be left alone.

'That's the whole trouble, you *don't* care,' Alex suddenly erupted, swinging away from her and marching across the room, and then turning back to face her. 'That's what this is all about. Any wife worth her salt would never have allowed another woman to climb into her husband's bed in the middle of the night.' A feral smile curved his lips. 'I am damned sure I would not stand by and let a man walk into your bed.'

She didn't doubt him for a moment. 'But then, as you and I both know, unlike you, I have never invited any man into my bed,' Lisa shot back.

'I'm thirty-five. Few men my age have led a celibate life,' Alex opined with a shrug of his broad shoulders. 'Margot meant nothing to me, though I will admit she should never have got in here tonight. I have spoken to Security, but unfortunately the man on duty this evening has just returned from a rather long absence from work because of ill health. The man knew Margot, and was not aware I had since married. A mistake he will not make again,' he declared. 'I will not tolerate anyone who harms you, directly or indirectly.'

His dark-lashed eyes glittered brilliantly on hers, and he lifted his hand to brush a stray tendril of hair gently back behind her ear. Lisa believed he meant what he said, but sadly she recognised it was not from love, but from his inbuilt male possessiveness. She was his wife, *ergo*, his property.

'You are my wife,' Alex continued huskily, 'and I can safely say from the minute I met you there has been no one else.'

Her blonde head flew back and she shook off his hand. 'Are you sure about that, Alex?'

'Of course. I do not lie.' If she hadn't known better, Lisa might almost have believed he was offended. He lifted his hand towards her again, and she stepped back a pace. His black eyes flared with some indefinable emotion which he then quickly masked, and his hand fell to his side. 'But perhaps now is not the time for this conversation. We are both tired and may say things we will regret. 'Suddenly he had gone all formal on her, his anger held in check. Only the tight line of his mouth betrayed his strict control.

'The only thing I regret is marrying you,' Lisa said bluntly. 'And by the way, Alex, I recognised your girl-friend. She was appearing at the theatre in Stratford on the evening we met. You must have spent that night with her and then called for me the next day.' She watched as a swift tide of colour swept up his face, turning his complexion a dark red. 'I'm not a fool, Alex, even if I have let you almost make one out of me. But not any more. Next you'll be telling me you forgot to ask for the key back,' she continued scathingly. 'You are certainly your father's son. Five times married, isn't it? Well, you can mark me down as your first. And start looking for the second. It is over. Finished.'

Alex stared at her in bitter, hostile silence for long moments. Then he stepped back. 'It is finished when I say so,' he informed her arrogantly 'I am not prepared to argue with you any longer. You can stay in here for what is left of the night. We will continue this discussion in the morning, when you have got over your sulk and are prepared to act like an adult.' Turning on his heel, he crossed to the door and opened it.

'As far as I am concerned, the discussion is over. I will be leaving in the morning,' she flung at his departing back.

Alex paused, then turned round and glanced at her, something dark leaping to life in his eyes. Lisa involuntarily stepped back, although he was nowhere near her. 'You are not leaving tomorrow, or any other day. Understood?' And before she could retaliate he walked out, banging the door behind him.

Shock and anger had kept her upright, but with Alex's departure she sank down on the bed and buried her head in the pillow. She wanted to scream and yell out her pain, but the lesson she had learned as a teenager, when her height had made her an outcast from her peer group, gave her the strength to control her emotions. She would not allow herself to show her pain or humiliation to Alex. But anyone glancing at her lying on the bed would have seen her slender body shaking as she wept silently.

All cried out, Lisa turned over on to her back, her throat dry and sore. She wiped her eyes on the sleeve of her robe, breathed deeply and tried to tell herself she would get over it. But she knew she would never recover from the hurt Alex had inflicted on her. She would never trust another man as long as she lived.

Sighing, she rolled off the bed and stood up. There was no point in trying to sleep; the scent of Alex lingered on her skin from their earlier lovemaking—no, not love, *sex*, she amended. Glancing out of the window, she saw it was dawn. She headed for the bathroom, and, slipping the robe off her shoulders, she stepped into the shower stall and turned on the water.

She shivered as the first drops hit her flesh. It was cold. Adjusting the temperature, she flung her head back and let the warm water flow over her. How long she stood like that she had no idea, but slowly a sense of purpose seeped into her tired mind. She shampooed and conditioned her long hair and then, picking up the shower gel, she scrubbed every single inch of her body in frenzied effort to remove every trace of Alex from her. She turned off the water and stepped out of the shower, collecting a large towel from the pile provided and rubbing herself dry.

Dropping the towel, she picked up the hairdryer and, standing in front of the vanity mirror, began blow-drying her hair. She studied her reflection, a grim travesty of a smile twisting her mouth; her skin was red from her efforts in the shower. It was a pity she could not wash Alex out of her mind as easily. But, given time, she would, Lisa vowed.

Grabbing another towel she wrapped it around herself. Her mind was made up: she was going back to Stratford and she was not waiting for another confrontation with Alex. She knew her own weakness too well. Alex was clever; he would talk her into staying and use sex to convince her. She had little faith in her power to resist him and she wasn't hanging around long enough to find out.

All her clothes were in the dressing room of the master

suite, but luckily the dressing room could be entered via the hall as well as the master bedroom. Slipping into the dressing room, she stopped and listened, but everywhere was silent. It took her no more than a minute to withdraw blue briefs and matching lace bra from a drawer and slip them on. Another minute, and she had silently opened the closet where she had hung her clothes and quickly stepped into light blue linen pants. Her head was lost in the folds of a navy cotton knit sweater when disaster struck.

'Lisa, your're not usually an early riser; that is my prerogative.' A deep, husky voice broke the silence, and two arms curved around her waist.

With her arms up in the air, stuck halfway into her sweater, Lisa was in a hopeless position. She felt his hands slide up over her midriff to cup her breasts over the flimsy lace of her bra. She drew in a shuddering breath and managed to wriggle her arms and head free of the restraining garment. 'Let go of me,' she snapped.

A throaty chuckle simmered along her throat as he nuzzled her neck, 'You don't mean that, Lisa. You smell so sweet, so delicious,' he husked, holding her firmly back against his hard thighs.

'And you are an oversexed jerk,' She spat, suddenly aware the beast was aroused, and, twisting around to face him, she splayed her hands over his broad chest and pushed with all her might. But it was like trying to fell an oak tree with her bare hands. Alex simply folded his arms around her taut body and held her pressed tightly to him.

'Now, is that any way to greet your husband?' he drawled mockingly.

'Soon to be ex-husband,' She replied pithily, her eyes skimming over him. He was wearing a white silk shirt, unbuttoned to the waist, and pleated beige pants.

Obviously he had not been lying in bed, as Lisa had hoped. She was uncomfortably aware he was fresh from the shower, his black hair damp, the clean, masculine scent of him filling her nostrils and, to her chagrin, she could feel her breasts swelling against the soft lace of her bra.

He studied her tousled appearance, her long blonde hair tumbling around her shoulders, her hands curled into fists on his broad chest. He took his time looking her over, a glint of devilment in his dark eyes. He knew perfectly well how he affected her. A broad grin curved his mouth, making her vitally aware of the sensuality lurking within his hard body. 'Come on, Lisa, where is your sense of humour? You don't want to leave,' he contradicted softly. His dark head lowered, his lips feathering across hers, and she shivered as the pressure of his kiss deepened, the hard heat of his mouth burning on her own.

Lisa groaned, caught in the trap of sensation much stronger than she was. How could it be? she thought helplessly, while every part of her burned in a fever of need.

'That is better.' Alex eased her away from him with a husky laugh. 'You look more like the girl I married. No more sulks, hmm?' He stepped back, his smile tinged with a glint of triumph.

It was his satisfaction that really got Lisa. Still reeling from the power of his kiss, she was jerked back to reality with a thump. 'I do not sulk, and I meant what I said, Alex. I want a divorce,'

He absorbed her flushed and angry face with arrogant detachment. 'No, you don't. You simply want to punish me for that unfortunate occurrence last night.'

'Unfortunate? I don't think so! Quite the reverse. It was fortunate for me.' Lisa flared. 'It showed me what a low-life I had married. And I want out.'

'Lowlife. Out,' Alex repeated, his eyes narrowed, his jaw clenching. 'No one talks to me like that. Not even you, my beautiful wife.' He told her icily.

'I mean it, Alex.' She defied him.

'Then, if that is so, I will be forced to do something about it.' The illusion of icy control was abruptly cast aside as strong hands curved around her forearms. 'No way are you walking out on our marriage after less than a month.'

'You can't stop me,' she said bluntly, but even so it took all her courage to stare bravely up into Alex's face.

'Oh, but I can.' A hard-boned savagery contorted his handsome features. 'You are mine, and mine you will stay until I decide otherwise.'

'Caveman tactics went out with the Dark Ages, Alex. Or hadn't you heard?' she hit back sarcastically, but inside she was quaking at the force of his rage.

'No.' His fingers held her tight. 'I am not letting you go until I get to the bottom of your outrageous behaviour. What do you take me for?'

He set her free and backed off a few steps, but his angry gaze held hers with narrow-eyed intensity. 'The truth is Lisa, this sudden desire to be single again is not just because of last night. The girl with whom I spent the last few weeks would have laughed off the episode, without a murmur. No. There is a hidden agenda here.'

'I don't know what you're talking about.' But she knew she sounded less than convincing. The thought of Alex's betrayal with Nigel lay heavily on her mind.

A black brow lifted sardonically. 'Oh, I think you do. But if you imagine I am parting with half a million pounds for barely a month in your bed, then forget it. You're good, but not that good.' And, turning around, he collected a jacket from the wardrobe and slipped it on.

Hectic colour tinged her cheeks; she had forgotten about the prenuptial agreement. 'That's a filthy thing to say, and utterly ridiculous.'

Slowly he turned back to face her. 'No more ridiculous than your demand for a divorce,' he whipped back derisively. 'I want the truth, Lisa, and I intend to get it.' With an angry glance around the small room, he added, 'But the dressing room is no place for a serious talk.' Taking her arm, he herded her through into the living area. Lisa was too surprised to object.

He'd had the audacity to suggest she was a gold-digger, when the reverse was true! But then, with her common sense returning, she recognised his ploy for what it was. A way of putting her on the defensive. Well, it was not going to work. When he pushed her down on to the leather sofa, she glared up at him with narrowed eyes. 'Think what you like, but it does not alter my position. I am leaving here today.'

Alex glanced at the watch on his wrist, and then at her flushed face. His dark eyes were calculatingly hard. 'I have a breakfast meeting, and not much time.'

'As soon as you leave, so shall I,' she asserted.

'You love your stepfamily. This I know.' A ruthless smile slanted his sensuous mouth. 'You stay here, or I will ruin them.'

She stared at him, her mind whirling. 'Why would you do that?' From what she had overheard, Nigel was in league with him, and personally Lisa didn't care if creepy Nigel fell flat on his face. But she did love Harold, and it might hurt him. Alex could certainly ruin Lawson's if he discovered she had given away her majority.

'Because, my sweet—' he glanced again at the slim gold watch on his wrist '—I have no more time to argue.'

Lisa couldn't take it in at first. *He had no time.* His

simple reason for threatening to destroy Nigel and Harold was all the more believable when he used that casual endearment. Even after last night, believing Alex had deceived her, she still had not quite believed the man she had married was so utterly and completely ruthless. But, looking up into his hard eyes, she realised he was not only serious but he was perfectly capable of doing what he said without a qualm of conscience. But then the man *had* no conscience.

'Have I made myself clear?' Alex drawled hardily.

'But what you're suggesting is despicable; it's nothing short of blackmail.'

'No worse than what you are trying to do. Our prenuptial gives you half a million for a month. No woman is worth that.'

'But I'm not. I didn't…' Lisa could not believe what was happening. He had turned the tables on her. She felt that she was in some nightmare, and that any second she would wake up and discover last night had never happened, or, better still, she amended, the last seven weeks had never happened.

'I have to return to Stratford today, to work,' she lied. Anything to get away.

'You do not. I had a long conversation with Harold last night. I know your second in command has taken over. There is no hurry for your return, and you have your laptop with you. Use the room you used last night as a study.' And, with another glance at his watch, he bent down and curved a large hand around her chin, and tilted her face up. His dark eyes lit with savage amusement. 'Try not to miss me too much, lover.'

Her furious blue eyes widened to their fullest extent. 'Why, you…you…' She could not think of a word bad enough to describe his sheer arrogance.

'Hush.' A finger was placed firmly across her lips. 'Do not incite my temper any further. You will not like the consequences.' he assured her, and then, as she watched, a wicked smile curved his hard mouth. 'But then again, you might enjoy it, if last night's seduction was a taste of what you are capable of.' With a husky laugh he released her chin.

Lisa blushed to the roots of her hair at his sensual reminder. She leapt to her feet. 'You can't order me around…'

'I can do anything, and don't you forget it,' he drawled his black eyes flashing a warning. 'Be here when I return, or it will be harder for you.'

'Wait.' She grabbed his arm. 'You can't make a statement like that and walk away.'

'Why not? It is no worse than you declaring you want a divorce and walking away.'

'But… But…' she stammered.

Lean fingers enclosed the hand she had laid on his arm. 'Not so nice, is it, Lisa? When the shoe is on the other foot? No?' And he actually laughed.

'You don't mean it,' she said uncertainly, as he slipped an arm around her waist, drawing her inexorably closer into the heat of his hard body. She was not sure if he was teasing or torturing her.

'Neither do you.' Folding both arms around her, his dark gaze steady on her troubled face, he added, 'Think about it from my point of view Lisa. Last night I fell asleep with my wife in my arms. You get up in the middle of the night, and another woman attempts to climb into our bed. Do you really think I am stupid enough to go to bed with one woman while waiting for another?'

She had trouble holding his gaze. His dark eyes bored into hers, and her own innate honesty forced her to admit that, if it had not been for the knowledge she had gained earlier about Nigel's involvement with Alex she probably would have stopped Margot at the door. 'I don't know,' she mumbled.

'Of course I am suspicious of the circumstances. But is your scenario any more valid? I think not,' he declared firmly.

'No,' Lisa conceded in defeat; she had to, unless she told him she knew about his plan to take over her company, and she was not ready to do that. She needed to make some investigations of her own first.

'Good, then let us make a pact, you and I. We will forget last night ever happened.'

'Very convenient for you,' Lisa could not help sniping.

'Come on, Lisa. Do you really want to go back and face your family and friends after a few short weeks, declaring your marriage to be over? Our wedding was reported in the press. Do you want to look a failure in the eyes of the world? More importantly, do you think for one minute I would allow you to make a failure out of me?' he demanded, with silken emphasis on the last question.

Lisa tensed, her slender frame taut as a bowstring, as she searched his darkly handsome face for any sign of weakness. There was none. Did she dare take a chance and defy him? More importantly, did she really want to?

'You are wise not to argue. This was our first fight, probably the first of many; you are a very feisty lady, which is why I adore you. But enough is enough, Lisa. Forget last night, and we start again from today,' he urged softly.

'Just like that?' Lisa shook her head at his arrogant conceit.

His dark head bent and he brought his mouth gently

down on hers. 'No, just like this.' He mouthed the words against her lips and then parted her lips to the seductive invasion of his tongue.

Heat coursed through her, and even as she knew she should resist a muffled whimper escaped her, and the familiar ache of longing arrowed through her body.

Alex only broke the kiss when she was utterly relaxed in his arms. 'If only I had time,' he murmured throatily, and raised his head to study her lovely face. His hand slid down to her buttocks and pressed her hard against his thighs, leaving her in no doubt about the potency of his masculine arousal.

Lisa was completely mesmerised by the desire in his dark eyes. She dragged in a ragged breath, fighting the pull of his attraction, but she did not need to. He flung his arms wide and stepped back.

'No more foolish talk of leaving, Lisa. You want me. I could have you now on the floor, and we both know it.' His dark eyes met and held hers, mutinously blue. 'And before you take off in another tantrum, know it is the same for me, Lisa.' His huskily voiced confession stopped the expletive she had been about to throw at him.

'It's just sex,' she muttered instead.

'Sex, love—call it what you will. But consider you may already be carrying our child.'

'I am not,' she shot back curtly. She had discovered the fact after her shower. 'I found that out as well.' To her utter astonishment Alex burst out laughing, his dark head thrown back, the morning sun streaming through the window glinting in the blue-black of his hair.

'Ah Lisa, now I understand. The wrong time of the month,' he chuckled, straightening his shoulders, his firm lips curving back over brilliant white teeth in a broad grin. 'Forget the foolishness of last night, sweetheart; I have.

You were not thinking logically; it is perfectly understandable in your condition.'

'My condition?' She spluttered, almost incandescent with rage. He actually thought her outburst was all down to PMT, the chauvinist. She could see it in his tender, patronising smile.

'Come, I can hear Mrs Blaydon arriving. She and her husband look after this place for me. I will introduce you, and then you go back to bed, rest. Leave everything to me.' With his hand at her elbow he urged her along towards the kitchen, and she was so speechless at his highhanded arrogance she let him!

CHAPTER FOUR

'IT IS a pleasure to meet you, Mrs Solomos.' The smiling, plump woman extended her hand to Lisa. 'I am so happy for you both, and if there is anything you want me to do for you, you only have to ask.' Smiling at Alex, she added, 'The coffee is fresh; what would you like to eat?'

'Just coffee, Mrs B; I have to dash. But I trust you to look after Lisa for me, and make sure she eats. She is feeling a bit tired today.' After downing the cup of coffee Mrs Blaydon had handed him he settled his dark gaze on Lisa. 'Come, walk me to the door. Mrs B understands. We are newlyweds,' he invited, his voice laced with a cynicism that only Lisa recognised as Mrs Blaydon chuckled with delight.

Alex's hand on the small of her back created a disturbing sensation that held a hidden warning; it also succeeded in fuelling her anger. 'I can walk,' she breathed in an undertone as they exited to the hall.

'So long as you know that you cannot walk out on me.' Alex's lazy reply only served to infuriate her further.

'You've made your point. I wouldn't dare.' Her head tilted fractionally and she met his dark gaze with clear control. 'Can I go and eat now?'

He lifted a hand and caught hold of her chin. 'Eat, yes. Go, no.' He stressed silkily, and his thumb traced a semi-circle up her chin, over her full lips and back down to slide to where the pulse beat heavily in her throat. 'Forget last night. Forget our fight. And remember only this appetite.' Alex tapped the pulse-beat in her throat, his head lowered and his lips brushed her cheek and the edge of her mouth. 'This appetite you and I will always share, Lisa.' She looked at him, the tug of sexual awareness impossible to deny. 'But do not underestimate me, Lisa. If I find you have betrayed my trust I can be a ruthless enemy, your worst nightmare.' It was the very softness of his tone that was enough to convince Lisa he was speaking the truth.

'And what of your betrayal?' she managed to retaliate.

Alex's eyes hardened fractionally. 'The question will not arise; you can trust me absolutely.' He caught hold of her hand and raised it to his lips. 'With this ring I thee wed' he repeated softly, and kissed the ring on her finger. 'I keep my promises. Be sure to keep yours, and we will have no more problems.' Dropping her hand, he also dropped a swift kiss on the top of her head. 'Rest. You look tired.'

'Thanks for the compliment.'

'Sarcasm does not become you, Lisa,' Alex opined dryly. 'See you tonight, and remember we are dining with my father.' Turning he opened the door and left.

Deprived of any chance to retaliate, she stood for a moment staring at the closed door. Alex was right in one respect. She did not relish the idea of returning home a failure, her marriage over after only a few weeks. Then there was still the problem of Nigel. It went against her nature to give in to blackmail, but it occurred to her that if Alex actually meant to destroy her stepfamily, that meant Harold. She could not keep Lawson's without Harold, so common sense told her she was better to stay where she was until she discovered exactly what was going on.

Lisa made her way back to the kitchen. Mrs Blaydon was putting toast in the electric toaster, and her smile was

warm as she watched Lisa walk over to the breakfast table
and sit down. Lisa filled a cup with coffee and took a
much needed drink of the reviving brew.

'Scrambled eggs on toast all right for you, Mrs
Solomos.'

Lisa replaced the cup on the table. 'Just toast, thanks.'

'Like my Bert; that's all he ever has.'

'Bert is your husband, then?' Lisa asked making idle
conversation, as the older woman placed a plate of toast
in front of her.

'Yes, married thirty-five years, and for the last fifteen
we have worked for Mr Alex. He was twenty-one and still
a student at university when he moved in here. He gave
Bert and I the apartment below, and we've looked after
the penthouse for him. He hasn't been around as much
the last few years, but he still keeps us on to take care of
all his visitors, and Bert acts as the official Solomos chauf-
feur when he's needed. Mr Alex usually drives himself,
but then the man does everything himself; he's a real
workaholic. Of course, that father of his is no help.
Always in the newspapers for all the wrong reasons.'

'I haven't actually met Alex's father yet. Apparently I
am to have that honour tonight,' Lisa cut in having finished her food.

'Some honour! The man hasn't done a hand's turn in
years, and yet to hear the old fool going on in the media,
he's a brilliant businessman. Brilliant is as brilliant does,
I say,' the housekeeper ended bluntly.

Lisa drained her coffee cup and stood up. 'Well, no
doubt I shall discover for myself tonight, but right now
I'd better get down to work.'

'Oh, no, you can't do any housework. That's my job.'

'Not housework.' Lisa corrected the housekeeper with
a smile. 'But I do run a business in Stratford-upon-Avon.

I've brought my computer with me, and I'm going to commandeer the first guest room for my office, if that's all right with you. Don't worry, Mrs Blaydon, I won't interfere with your work. Why don't you finish up here? It's a beautiful sunny day; you and Bert can have the day off.'

'Well, if you're sure.' Mrs Blaydon's pleasure was evident.

'Yes.' Lisa smiled, getting to her feet. 'But if you'll excuse me, I'd better get to work.'

In a matter of minutes she was seated at the desk in the room where she had spent the night, her laptop on, planning her defence. Buying the Lee shares was her safest option, but it didn't take Lisa long to realise she was paper rich but cash poor. Next, she checked everywhere she could think of to find the name of the company that had made the offer to buy Lawson's before her mother died. If she needed a white knight to help her fight off Alex's takeover attempt, that bidder seemed a good bet. At least that company hadn't wanted to flatten the place. After an hour she gave up in disgust. Perhaps the letter of refusal had never been filed on the computer; given the shock of her mother's illness at the time, it wasn't surprising. It would have to wait until she got back to the office on Monday, it might be in her mother's private papers, and Lisa was the only one with access to them.

As the morning progressed, Lisa fought against recalling last night's events, but she failed. She was mulling over her own ambivalence about the situation when Mrs Blaydon burst into the room, closely followed by two men.

'I was on my way out when these two men arrived. It's for you, from Mr Alex.'

'That's fine, Mrs Blaydon.' She watched the old

woman scurry off with a smile on her face. To say Lisa
was astonished was an understatement. Alex had sent her
a state-of-the-art computer, and the accompanying card
read. 'I hope this will keep you at home.'

Lisa shared a smile with the two young delivery men,
and watched with close attention as they installed the new
computer. Later, she set about E-mailing Mary, and then
Jed. Then she broke off for a coffee. Returning half an
hour later, she got the shock of her life when she clicked
on and a disembodied female voice declared, 'You have
mail.' Her old computer hadn't got a voice facility and
she was fascinated by it.

The E-mail was a reply from Mary. *'Congrats: but I
still think diamonds are a girl's best friend.'* Chuckling
to herself, Lisa spent the rest of the morning thoroughly
absorbed in her work. It was only when her stomach rumbled and she glanced at the time in the corner of the screen
that she realised the morning had gone.

She couldn't resist one more visit to the Internet, and
was rewarded with 'You have mail'. As it was the afternoon in the UK, it had to be early morning in Montana,
from where Jed was replying.

*'You lucky lady. The computer sounds great, but do I
detect a trace of coolness in your attitude to the giver,
and so soon??? Correct me if I am wrong. I'll get back
to you later. I have to go milk the cows.'*

Something in the tone of her message must have given
him an insight into her confused state of mind. That was
just so Jed. For a man she had never actually met, he had
an amazing sensitivity where she was concerned. She sent
a brief reply: *'Stick to analysing the cows, farm boy. I'm
fine.* A glimmer of a genuine smile brightened her face as

she closed down the computer and wandered back through the apartment to the kitchen.

Lisa made herself a cheese sandwich and, filling a glass with milk, she placed it and the plate on a tray and took her late lunch out to the rooftop garden. It was a gorgeous sunny afternoon, and, placing the tray on a Victorian wrought-iron table, she sat down on one of the matching chairs and picked up one half of her sandwich.

She munched her food without really tasting it, her mind awash with conflicting thoughts. She glanced at the gold watch on her wrist; it read slightly after three o'clock. Alex wouldn't be back before five-thirty at the earliest. There was still time for her to leave. But did she really want to? she asked herself. And, much as she hated to admit her weakness, the answer was no. The trouble was, she realised Alex the man she had married, was not the man she'd thought he was. She had never really known him…

She had always recognised Alex had a ruthless streak in him. He wouldn't be a success in the business world without a certain killer instinct to succeed. But, naively perhaps, she had never expected that side of his nature to be turned on her.

Even now she was not convinced he had meant his threat. He had said they would make a pact to start again, and by her silence she had given her agreement.

She could almost forgive him Margot's amazing intrusion last night. Her lips twitched in the beginnings of a smile. Alex's face had been a picture of outraged horror when she had clicked the light on and he had realised it was Margot climbing into their bed! He could not have faked his expression in a million years. He was usually so self-possessed—even in the throes of passion he never totally lost control.

Passion. That was another problem. Lisa had decided to stay, but was she prepared to crawl back into bed with Alex? The next week was taken care of; he wouldn't bother her knowing she had her period.

A deep sigh escaped her and, arching her back to get the tension out of her shoulders, she picked up the glass of milk and drained it, before replacing it on the tray. Then she stood up and carried the lot back to the kitchen. Lounging around the roof garden solved nothing, she told herself firmly. Action was what was needed.

Half an hour later Lisa was standing in the hall, a pile of clothes topped with lacy underwear in her arms, as she tried to push open the guest bedroom door with her rear.

'What the devil....?' Alex was walking towards her discarding his tie in the process, and looking distinctly puzzled.

'You're back early,' she said inanely, and met his dark gaze with a frown, her eyes lingering on the chiselled features and settling briefly on his mouth. Which was a mistake. He was tight-mouthed with anger.

'No, just in time, it would seem. Care to explain what you are doing? Or shall I guess,' he drawled cynically, moving to stand inches from her. His hand plucked a pair of crimson lace briefs off the top of the pile of clothes she was carrying, and swung the offending garment back and forth on one long finger.

He had caught her at a disadvantage, with her back to the door and her hands full. She had nowhere to go. 'Put them back,' she muttered, the colour rising in her cheeks, and she knew her face must almost match the briefs.

'I think that is my line, Lisa.' A faint smile tugged the edges of his mouth, but the expression in his eyes was still totally cynical. 'That room is your study, nothing more. So try acting like an adult instead of a spoilt child and return these.' He dropped the red briefs back on to the pile of clothes. 'Back to where they belong, in the master suite. I thought we had settled our differences this morning. I hope I was not wrong?' Shrugging out of his jacket, he hooked it over one shoulder and with his free hand began unbuttoning the first few buttons of his shirt.

He was too close, his height and wide shouldered frame intimidating. Her gaze slipped to the broad expanse of his tanned chest, and Lisa felt the familiar flood of warmth weaken her defences. She fought against it and, glancing up, her eyes met his. He knew how he affected her, at least on a sexual level, but to her surprise a tender smile curled his mouth.

'Sometimes I forget how innocent you are,' Alex murmured, and trailed a long finger over her burning cheek.

She felt about two inches tall, and totally foolish. She had decided to stay with Alex, but no way was she climbing meekly back into bed with him. 'Not any more,' she said bitterly, 'you saw to that.'

'Hush.' He pressed a finger to her lips. 'Allow me to apologise. You should never have been subjected to what happened last night. The lady had no right to intrude on our privacy, and it was unkind of me to even hint that you were in any way at fault. As your husband, it is my duty to protect you from any embarrassment, and I singularly failed to do so.' With the pad of his finger he flicked her bottom lip before dropping his hand to his side. 'Please forgive me.'

Lisa's mouth fell open and her blue eyes widened to their fullest extent on his serious face. Alex apologising and begging forgiveness? She could hardly believe it.

'Forgive you?' she parroted.

'Yes, ' he said simply. 'I should have realised you, with your lack of experience of predatory females who are all too common in the world, were in no position to argue with a woman like Margot. The golden purity that drew me to you in the first place should have reminded me of the fact. So, once again, am I forgiven?'

His deep velvet voice flowed like honey over her raw nerves, and in a voice she hardly recognised as her own, Lisa said, 'Yes, apology accepted.' In that moment she would have forgiven him murder. His body moved in close against her own, his dark head bent and he angled a kiss across her open lips, a kiss of tenderness and gentle possession.

Lisa stared up into his sexy, slumberous eyes as he raised his head and moved back a pace. 'Thank you, Lisa.' he husked.

Fighting down the urge to fling her arms around him—an impossible action given she was still holding a pile of garments, she realised, glancing down at her overloaded arms—she was suddenly aware of where she was and what she had been doing, and she stumbled into speech. 'Actually, it is I who should thank you. The computer is brilliant; it was good of you to buy it for me, but no need.' She was babbling, but couldn't seem to stop.

'Enough, sweetheart.' Alex grinned, and with a toss of his dark head he indicated the door opposite. 'After you.'

Her nervous tension dissolved and, taking a deep breath, she slipped past him and into the dressing room. Alex confounded and confused her, and retreat seemed the best option, but that did not mean she was going to crawl back into bed with him. Moving swiftly, she quickly placed the lingerie and clothes in the requisite drawers and the closet. His apology, she knew, was genuine, but it did not alter the fact he was about to betray her, by dealing with Nigel. Perhaps that was the difference between men and women, Lisa thought sadly. Men could separate business completely from their emotional life.

Lisa, unfortunately, could not. By the same token, she knew she would never agree to Lawson's being flattened to make way for something else. It was her parents' memorial. Maybe that made her a poor businesswoman, but she did not care. There had to be more to life than simply the pursuit of riches. But she had a growing conviction her husband did not share her view.

Reluctantly she walked back into the bedroom; she heard the sound of the shower from the *ensuite* bathroom and heaved a sigh of relief. She didn't have to face Alex again just yet; a glance at her watch told her it was five. Time to have a cup of tea and restore her equilibrium before she got ready for the evening ahead.

'Pour me a cup,' Alex commanded, and Lisa almost dropped the teapot. He had showered and shaved and was sporting a pair of well-washed jeans and nothing else.

'I didn't think you drank tea?' she murmured.

Pulling out a chair opposite her he sat down. 'If you do, I do. It is part of marriage, the sharing.' Alex's faintly accented statement had a mocking edge as he reached out and accepted the cup she had automatically filled for him.

'Yes, yes, I suppose so,' she acknowledged.

'Which is why I thought, tomorrow, you and I could spend the day in the countryside. I had my people get on to some real estate agents while we were away, and they have come up with a couple of quite decent looking properties.'

'Properties? You mean houses?'

'But of course.' And with a brief glance around the kitchen Alex returned his attention to her puzzled face. 'This place is adequate in the short term, but obviously we will need a family home. Knowing you as I do the country is the answer, I think.'

Lisa sipped her tea, unsure of how to respond. She had always lived in a large house on the outskirts of Stratford-upon-Avon; she had only to walk out of her garden to take a stroll along country lanes. Alex was right; she did prefer the country. But what of Alex? While not notorious as an international jet-setter like his father, she wasn't sure she could see him as a country squire. 'Do you actually have a proper home?' she surprised herself by asking. 'I mean, apart from here?'

His black eyes twinkled with laughter. 'I hate to spoil my image, but in fact I actually still live with my mother. Officially my residence is the villa on Kos. The yacht is berthed in the harbour there, and whenever I have time I go back home. Otherwise I tend to stay in an apartment the company owns, or a hotel.'

'Of course!' Lisa exclaimed. 'I should have guessed the villa we stayed in when we visited your mother was yours.' She remembered thinking at the time that the sitting room and bedroom of their suite had had a very lived-in feel about them; the pictures on the walls had been mostly of boats—a hobby of Alex's—and there had been a couple of trophies for yacht racing that had borne Alex's name. For a few timeless seconds her eyes locked with his and they shared a mutual memory of a night spent in sheer bliss.

'Yes,' Alex confirmed, his eyes sweeping over her shoulders and the curve of her breast before returning to study the surprised and faintly embarrassed expression on her delicately etched features. A smile quirked the corner of his mouth. 'But now I think I am old enough to own my home,' he teased. 'Don't you agree?'

Lisa couldn't disagree without getting into a morass of

lies. The truth was not an option. She was waiting to see
if Alex was going to betray her, along with her stepbrother. She gave the only answer she could think of.
'Yes, well,' she qualified, 'we will see.' And, pushing
back her chair and getting to her feet, she added, 'But
right now I'd better get dressed. What time did you say
we were meeting your father?'

Only the slight narrowing of his dark eyes gave away
the fact her evasion had been noted and disliked, but,
rising to his feet, he said, 'Seven or seven-thirty. I have
a few calls to make in my study. I won't be long.'

The bathroom off the master bedroom was almost as
big as the bedroom itself. Elegantly designed and con-
structed in pale pink streaked marble, it held a large double shower and a circular spa bath. Plus all the usual fa-
cilities. The lingering scent of Alex hung on the air,
making her catch her breath.

She did not linger in the shower and, as she had washed
her hair that morning, five minutes later she entered the
dressing room, a towel wrapped around her slender
curves, and selected fresh briefs and quickly slipped them
on.

Seated at the dressing table, she twisted the long length
of her hair into a high pleat on the back of her head. With
the deft use of a few pins, she quickly had a very fash-
ionable hairstyle. She pulled a few tendrils of hair loose
around her face and the back of her neck and surveyed
the finished result. Sophisticated, but not too contrived,
she thought, and then began applying her make-up.

Rising to her feet, she crossed to the cupboards that ran
the full length of two walls.

Sliding open one of the doors, she withdrew the gown
she had hung there the night before, ready for this evening's dinner party. She eyed the dress with dismay.

When she had bought it in a boutique in Stratford she had thought it was perfect, with stiletto-heeled evening shoes and a purse dyed to match. The whole ensemble was suitable for a sophisticated lady wanting to seduce her husband. Now she was not so sure. But realistically she had nothing else; the clothes she had packed were day and casual wear. So, unless she wanted to meet Alex's father in trousers or a business suit, she had no choice.

She stepped into the blue gown and pulled the zip up its side. It was a simple sheath; the bodice had a bra built in and was cut straight across her breasts in a band of delicately beaded embroidery, revealing the soft swell of her breasts. The rest stuck to her like a second skin, to end some six inches above her knees in another band of beading. She slipped her feet into the shoes, then quickly slipped pearl studs into her ear lobes, and fastened the matching string of pearls around her throat. She dabbed some of her favourite perfume behind her ears and the back of her knees. Straightening, she turned towards the mirror to cast her reflection a brief glance.

'Wow, that is some dress.'

Lisa turned at the sound of Alex's voice, and felt her breath catch at the image he presented. He was still only wearing jeans, and his hand had obviously been ruffling his hair, but there was something about his stance, a sense of predatory strength as his dark eyes swept down over her curvaceous body and lingered for an instant on the long length of her legs before returning to her face. The deepening gleam of sexual desire turned his eyes to black as they clashed with hers.

'Maybe we should forget dinner,' Alex murmured, stepping towards her, his intention obvious.

'You'd better hurry up and get dressed, or we'll be

late,' she retaliated, as she deftly sidestepped around him. He stopped her with a hand on her arm.

'Your're right; I got trapped on the telephone. Be a sweetheart and mix me a whisky and soda. I have a feeling I am going to need it tonight.'

'What about driving?' she murmured.

'Bert is driving us there, and we will grab a taxi back; no need for the old boy to have a late night.'

A few minutes later, she walked back into the bedroom, a glass of whisky and soda in her hand. She stopped inside the door. Alex was slipping on the jacket of his dinner suit, and he turned at her entrance.

'Thanks, Lisa.' He moved to her side and took the glass from her hand; his fingers brushed hers and sent a swift jolt of electricity up her arm. He was devastatingly attractive at any time, but wearing a superbly cut dinner suit, with his black hair slicked back from his broad forehead, he exuded an aura of powerful male magnetism that few men possessed. She watched as he raised the glass to his mouth and drained it. She was fascinated by the way his strong tanned throat moved when he swallowed, and only realised she was staring when he spoke.

'Come on, Lisa, we're cutting it fine as it is.'

At the hotel the doorman opened the car door almost before it had stopped. Taking a deep breath, Lisa alighted with some elegance, and before she could even take a step Alex was at her side, his hand under her elbow to guide her inside…

CHAPTER FIVE

WALKING from the brightness of the fine June evening into the darkened interior of the hotel Lisa was blinded for a second, and she stumbled slightly. Alex tightened his grip on her arm.

'You did not hit the whisky as well, I hope,' he quipped, his dark eyes laughing down at her in easy intimacy.

The charm of his smile squeezed her heart. 'No,' she snapped, scared by the emotion he could so easily arouse in her. 'Though being blackmailed by one's husband is reason enough for anyone to hit the bottle,' she informed him with sweet sarcasm.

'Blackmailed?' His brows drew together in a frown. 'Ah, you mean your beloved stepfamily. I was in a hurry this morning and I said the first thing that came into my head.'

'So you say,' she murmured. 'But it worked. I'm here at your side instead of at home in Stratford.' She didn't know why she was needling him, and as for her stepfamily, Nigel was certainly not her beloved anything…

'Your home is with me,' Alex said, his grip on her arm tightening. 'Now drop this stupid conversation. This evening—' He stopped in mid-sentence. Lisa followed the direction of his gaze and felt her heart sink in her chest.

Some thirty feet away but moving towards them was a tall, overweight, grey-haired man. The family likeness was unmistakable; it had to be Alex's father. By his side was a young woman, dark-haired and beautiful, thirty-something, and moreover someone Lisa had met before.

'Damn, I thought I had frightened the woman off,' Alex swore, his dark eyes narrowing intently on the approaching couple.

Lisa straightened her shoulders and shrugged off Alex's supporting hand. 'Obviously not. Fiona Fife, I believe, another one of your lady-friends.' She was determined to act the sophisticate tonight in front of Alex and his father, but she had a horrible feeling it was not going to be so easy, especially if she was going to keep bumping into her husband's mistresses at every turn!

Alex glanced at her, his dark eyes clashing with her angry blue. 'I do believe you're jealous,' he prompted softly.

Lisa gave a slight shrug, pretending indifference. 'Should I be?' she asked lightly, and held his gaze with difficulty.

'No. You are the only girl for me, darling, plus I am not old enough for that particular lady,' he drawled mockingly, with a brief glance at the other couple. Tilting his head towards Lisa, he added, *sotto voce*, 'It is my father she has designs on. She is hopeful of becoming wife number six. Our Italian friend informed me of that at that party we attended in Monte Carlo. I did try to warn her off, with tales of his weak heart and nowhere near as much money as she imagines, but it looks like I failed.' His firm mouth twisted in a wry grimace. 'Not for the first time, unfortunately.'

Inexplicably, Lisa's spirits lifted considerably at his words. Now she knew why he had danced with the woman when they were on their honeymoon, and somehow it made her feel a whole lot better.

'Brace yourself, here they come.' Alex slid his arm

around her waist and urged her forward. 'Father,' he greeted the older man warmly. 'It's been a while.'

'Indeed it has,' the older man agreed. 'You've met Fiona?' He indicated the woman at his side, and both Alex and Lisa gave a social smile and said hello to the black-haired beauty.

'And this must be your wife.' Mr Solomos senior's dark eyes were so like his sons as he scrutinised Lisa from head to toe, and then he broke out into a broad grin. 'Charming, absolutely beautiful. Though you could have told me, Alex. I thought I was the only one who married quickly in our family. Obviously you have inherited some of my traits after all.'

She felt Alex stiffen at her side but, ignoring his father's comment he simply said, 'Lisa, allow me to introduce you to my father, Leo, and don't be taken in by his charm; it is his stock-in-trade.'

Lisa held out her hand and the old man engulfed it in his. He looked like Alex, though he was a few inches shorter, but he did not have the same aura of compelling dynamism that Alex possessed in such abundance.

'How do you do?' she said formally, and felt the colour rise in her face when Leo laughed out loud.

'So formal, so very English. I hope you are a match for my son's fiery Greek temperament.'

'Lisa is a perfect match in every way,' Alex informed him, subjecting Lisa to a slow, sensual appraisal that left no one in any doubt of exactly what he meant.

His father chuckled again. 'I'm glad to hear it.' Turning to Fiona with a smile, he demanded, 'Shall we tell them?'

Fiona's eyes lifted to Alex, the smile on her perfectly made-up face one of triumph. 'Oh, yes, I think your son and his wife—' she glanced briefly at Lisa, but immediately turned her attention back to Alex '—should be the first to know.'

'Fiona and I are flying to Las Vegas tomorrow afternoon to get married.'

Was the old man aware of the effect he had on his son? Lisa wondered. She felt Alex's fingers dig into her side, and the increased tension in his body, but not by a flicker of an eyelash did he display his concern.

'Congratulations appear to be in order all round,' Alex offered, his eyes narrowing fractionally on his father. 'I trust everything else is in order also.'

Watching him, Lisa actually felt some pity for her husband in that moment. Having met his mother, and seen the love and affection between them, she realised how hard it must be for him when he was about to gain stepmother number five!

'Yes, Alex, I visited Mr Niarchos this morning. He will be in touch tomorrow.'

Lisa felt the tension drain out of Alex, and his hand at her waist relaxed slightly.

'Good,' he agreed urbanely. 'Shall we forgo drinks and go into dinner?'

A slight frown of puzzlement creased Lisa's smooth brow. There was obviously more being said between the two men than the words they spoke revealed. Then it hit her—the mention of the lawyer. Alex was checking his father had made a prenuptial agreement. How sad... But it was nothing to do with her, she told herself, as she walked towards the dining room at her husband's side. She couldn't help being aware of the intense interest their foursome aroused in the hotel's clientele. Mostly down to Alex; she had no illusions on that score. He was an exceptionally impressive man.

The restaurant was filled with customers, but Leo had

booked ahead, and the *maître d'* greeted him with the familiarity of an old friend. They were directed to a table and a waiter appeared at Leo's side in a second, quickly followed by the wine waiter.

The best champagne was requested, and Leo ordered for Fiona without bothering to ask. Alex ordered a Waldorf salad for starters, followed by steak and fresh fruit, but at least he had the manners to ask Lisa what she preferred. She selected the pâté and opted for the fillet of trout garnished with prawns and melted butter. Hiding a smile, she recognized Alex had inherited his chauvinistic traits from his father...

'You're not watching your figure, then, Lisa?' Fiona queried, in the first sentence she had addressed to Lisa. 'But then of course you have never been a model. I have to be so body-conscious; everything must be perfect.' And with a simpering glance at Leo and a hand on his arm she concluded, 'But that is how Leo likes me.'

From the lecherous look on the old man's face as he stared at Fiona's cleavage—she was wearing a white slip dress that plunged to her waist back and front—Leo would have preferred her like Lisa's trout: naked but for a covering of butter, Lisa thought dryly, before responding, 'I'm sure he does.' She paused for a second, stumped for something else to say. She knew she had just been insulted, but she was too polite to retaliate.

The arrival of the waiter with the bottle of champagne was a timely interuption. The waiter filled all four glasses, and Leo raised his first.

'A toast to the newlyweds, Alex and Lisa. And the soon to be wed, Fiona and myself.'

Lisa lifted her glass and sipped the sparkling champagne; she touched glasses with the couple sitting opposite.

'And your husband,' Alex murmured.

It was a rectangular table, with Leo next to Fiona and Alex at her side. She turned her head slightly towards him and touched her glass to his. 'Of course, my husband,' she conceded with a smile, opting for a casual response. There were enough undercurrents of tension in the atmosphere without her adding to it by arguing with Alex.

'To my darling wife.' Alex held her gaze for a few heart-stopping seconds, his eyes darkening sensually with muted desire. She knew he was doing it deliberately, but she still had to fight to control the sudden upsurge in her pulse rate, and hastily took a deep drink of the wine and looked away.

Surprisingly, Leo Solomos turned out to be a witty, convivial host. He asked Lisa about her work and family, and congratulated her on her business acumen. The food was cooked to perfection and Lisa slowly began to relax. In fact she discovered she quite enjoyed the company. Though when Leo tried to fill her glass for the fourth time, she refused.

Three bottles of champagne were consumed, and Lisa couldn't help thinking that for a woman who was so bothered about her appearance, Fiona could certainly down her drink. The only time the conversation flagged was when Fiona spoke. She seemed to have a perfect memory for every modelling assignment she had ever been on, and complete recall of every gown she'd worn. Thankfully, Leo had the happy knack of distracting her by placing a finger on her lips or with a kiss.

Alex on the other hand, played the part of the perfect husband, with reassuring smiles for Lisa or a quick aside to enquire if she was okay. By the time dessert arrived Lisa was happy to concede that Leo was a charming man.

His only fault appeared to be his penchant for young women.

She had just stopped laughing at Leo's tall tale about a donkey that snored, on the island of Kos, and was about to resume eating her fruit salad, when a disturbing realisation hit her like a blow to the stomach. She replaced her spoon in the dish and pushed it away; she could not eat another thing.

'What is the matter?' Alex demanded, turning slightly in his seat, his dark head angled towards her. 'The fruit is not to your liking?' His thoughtful gaze searched her suddenly pale face, and she realised her husband was a very astute man; he saw far too much.

She forced a smile to her lips. 'No, it's fine, but, really, I've had enough.' More than enough, she thought with a heavy heart. It had suddenly occurred to her the friendly smiling Leo opposite was not just Alex's father, he was also his business partner. If Alex was trying to take over her company, then obviously his father was aware of the situation. The older man's good humour and friendly interest about Lisa's work were as false as the marriage vows he kept repeating...

'Are you sure?' Alex insisted, placing a finger under her chin and turning her head to face him. She was unaware of the pain shadowing her blue eyes, but it was apparent to Alex. 'You're tired and not quite yourself; I forgot,' he murmured huskily, as he smoothed his finger down her throat. Her pulse leapt at his touch and he noted the fact with a slight twist to his sensual mouth.

'We can leave now, if you like,' he prompted softly. 'An early night would suit both of us.'

'No, no I'm fine.' Lisa confirmed, forcing a smile.

Thankfully, the waiter arrived at that moment, and Leo demanded quite loudly, 'We will have coffee in the lounge. I don't enjoy a meal without a good cigar afterwards.'

Seated next to Alex on a low leather sofa, his arm casually placed around her shoulders, his fingers on her flesh playing havoc with her nervous system, Lisa chewed on her bottom lip, torn between wanting the evening to end and anxiety about being alone with Alex again. When the waiter deposited the coffee tray on the low table in front of them Lisa leant forward, displacing Alex's arm, and took a cup of coffee from the tray before the waiter had a chance to hand it to her. Lounging on the sofa to the left of her was Leo, a huge cigar clamped between his teeth, and the stomach-curling smell as he blew smoke out was making her feel sick. At least that was what she told herself as she quickly drained her coffee cup and leapt to her feet, excusing her departure with the need to visit the rest room.

In the cool confines of the marble-walled room, she heaved a sigh of relief. But it was short-lived, as Fiona walked in. With a brief smile at the other woman, Lisa opened her purse and withdrew a lipgloss. She eyed her reflection in the mirror; there was nothing in her expression, she thought gratefully, that revealed the fraught state of her emotions. The social mask was still in place, and carefully she outlined her full mouth with the rose gloss.

'Funny to think after this weekend I will be your stepmother-in-law,' Fiona remarked, standing beside Lisa at the mirror, primping her dark hair. Her brown eyes clashed with Lisa's in the mirror. 'And I'm only a year or so older than you.'

More like ten, Lisa thought, but didn't say so. 'Yes, well, I don't suppose you'll want me to call you Mum.' She responded with a tinge of sarcasm. She found it very hard to believe Fiona was marrying Leo for any other reason but money.

'Good God! No! But there's no reason why we can't be friends, you and I, after all, we have a lot in common,' Fiona said with a smug grin. 'The way you hooked Alex was absolutely brilliant.'

'The way I hooked Alex?' Lisa prompted, her blue eyes puzzled. She had not 'hooked Alex'; it had been the other way round.

Oblivious to Lisa's surprise, Fiona carried on, 'So quickly. I couldn't have done better myself. Well, I didn't, did I?' She grimaced. 'But I've got Leo. Though I don't mind admitting when I met the pair of them in March, at Leo's sixtieth birthday in Nice, I had every intention of going after Alex. It was obvious to me—feminine intuition, if you like—that he was fast losing interest in that Margot creature. He was distinctly cool towards her. No, if I hadn't had to go to the Caribbean on a modelling assignment, I would have given you a run for your money over Alex. Still, Leo's not too bad—and, let's face it, they're both as rich as Croesus.'

'But surely you must love Leo,' Lisa prompted. To think a woman was marrying for money was one thing; to be told she was seemed quite extraordinary to Lisa.

'Oh, I do. I love his money, and he's not a bad old stick.' With a last casual flick at her hair she turned to leave. 'Come on, we'd better get back. You can't leave a couple of wealthy men like those two on their own for too long, there are a lot of predatory women out there.'

Lisa chuckled; she couldn't help herself. Anyone more predatory than Fiona would be hard to find. She followed the other woman back to the lounge and her blue-eyed gaze instinctively settled on Alex.

He was the epitome of male sophistication, lounging

back on the deep leather sofa, his long legs stretched out before him in casual ease. The man was sinfully attractive. A tiny shiver of excitement quivered deep inside. And, as she knew only too well, he was a deeply passionate and wickedly sensual lover. Fiona was wrong about the pulling power of the Solomos wealth, she thought, a wry smile curving her mouth as Alex stood up at her approach. He could be a pauper and he would still have women falling at his feet.

'You're smiling; you must be feeling better.' Dark eyes scrutinised her slightly flushed face. 'But I think it is time we left.' He lifted a large tanned hand and let his fingertip trace the purple shadows under her eyes in a fleeting gesture that made her whole body tense. 'Okay?'

Lisa looked up into his eyes, the smile fading from her face. It wasn't okay, but she really had no alternative. 'Yes,' she agreed, and managed not to flinch when his dark head lowered and he pressed the lightest of kisses on her soft lips.

After reiterating their congratulations on Leo's forthcoming nuptials, they said goodnight and left.

Lisa stepped outside into the mild night air, and took a deep breath to clear her head and to steady her wildly fluctuating emotions. She loved Alex; he only had to look at her and she ached for him. To deny him was to deny herself the wonder of his lovemaking, the pleasure she found in his arms. Yet she no longer trusted him.

The doorman was holding open the door of a black cab and Alex, with a hand in the small of her back, was urging her forward. She slid along the seat and Alex followed, casually placing a long arm around her slender shoulders. She immediately shuffled further along the seat. Alex cast her a sidelong glance, one brow arched quizzically, but he made no comment as he simply hauled her back against him. Leaning forward, he instructed the driver on their destination.

The warmth of his large male body, the subtle scent of his cologne all conspired to break down her reservations about their relationship. As Alex sat back, his glance lingered for a moment on the long length of her legs. She attempted to pull the hem of her dress lower and he chuckled, leaning his head back against the seat.

'You did that the very first time I set eyes on you. Not still shy, Lisa?' he teased.

'Not at all,' she denied, but felt foolish. But then most women were foolish where love was concerned, she thought sadly, unless one happened to be like the Fionas of this world; unfortunately for Lisa, she wasn't. Sighing, she let her head fall back; she was tired, and with Alex's warm hand cupping her bare shoulder, his thumb gently kneading the back of her neck, she gradually felt the tension ease from her body. Why fight it? she asked herself. If Alex had married her to get Lawson's, she would find out soon enough. Meanwhile, why not enjoy her marriage while it lasted? After Alex she knew she would never marry any another man. A soft sigh escaped her and she allowed her head to rest on his broad shoulder, and he held her in a comfortable silence as the cab navigated the London streets.

It was only when they entered the private elevator which would take them to the penthouse that Lisa felt the tension returning. She glanced at Alex as he pressed the requisite button and the metal doors slid shut, closing them into the luxuriously carpeted box. 'How do you feel about your father's up-coming marriage?' she asked, more to break the silence than out of any real curiosity, as the elevator whisked them ever nearer the apartment, and the bedroom...

Alex flicked her a glance. 'Don't be concerned; I am not,' he drawled in a dry, mocking tone. 'I gave up worrying about my father years ago.'

'You don't mind he's marrying a woman younger than you.'

'Why should I? We will hardly ever see them,' Alex responded dismissively.

The elevator doors swung open and she flinched as Alex reached for her arm and guided her across the hallway to the apartment. 'But he is your father...' she insisted.

'Drop it,' he snapped as he opened the door and ushered her into the apartment.

'Aren't you worried about him? You must care for him.'

Closing the door behind him, Alex said bluntly, 'It is really not your concern, Lisa. Now, do you want a nightcap, or shall we go straight to bed?'

His response simply confirmed her judgement of the man. Alex did not even care for his father, so what hope had she of him genuinely caring for her? None! She didn't want a drink, but neither did she want to go to bed—at least not with Alex. Or so she told herself. 'I'll have a very small cognac.'

Dropping her purse on the hall table, she kicked off her shoes before following him into the living room. She watched as he crossed to the drinks cabinet and poured a small amount of cognac into a crystal glass, and then twice as much of the liquor into another glass. Turning around, he closed the distance between them, a glass in each hand. He held out the smaller measure to her. As she took it, her fingers brushed against his.

She resented the way a simple touch set her pulse racing, and, glancing up at him, she resented even more the way he knew exactly how she felt. She wanted to rage at him, demand to know about his deal with Nigel. She needed to know the truth. But she could not bring herself to ask.

'You look angry,' he observed with narrowed eyes. 'And there is no need. My father is perfectly able to look after himself.' Lifting his glass to his mouth, he drained it, then placed it on the table. 'But perhaps it is not my father's wedding that has angered you. Perhaps something else,' he mused. 'You're not still thinking of last night's farce? I thought we had settled that,' he declared, eyeing her speculatively.

'No,' she swiftly denied, and in truth Nigel, not Margot, was behind her simmering anger. 'I'm simply amazed you can dismiss your father's marriage so lightly.' Tossing back her head, she swallowed the cognac in one go.' Leaning forward, she deposited her glass on the table. Straightening up, she realised he had moved closer. But he made no attempt to touch her.

'Somehow, I don't think my father is the real reason for all the latent anger that shimmers in your expressive eyes, nor do I think it is because of Margot's untimely intrusion into our life. So, I have to ask myself, what exactly is it that you are hiding?' he queried silkily.

He was too close, in more ways than one. The ease with which he had seen through her attempts to hide the real reason for her anger was worrying. 'I'm not hiding anything.' Lisa paused, then added with a flash of inspiration, 'Unless you consider a conversation with your future stepmother in the rest room a secret.'

He tipped his arrogant head back, a dangerous gleam lighting his dark eyes. 'Fiona? Explain,' he commanded hardly.

'Well, according to Fiona, she and I are very alike, and

if she hadn't had to go on a modelling assignment after your father's sixtieth birthday party she would now be your girlfriend. Fiona congratulated me on how quickly I nipped in and…' She hesitated delicately, the beginnings of a smile twitching her lips. She could see Alex detested the idea of women discussing him in the ladies' room, and she began to enjoy herself.

'Now, let me think. I believe ''hooked'' was the term she used. Apparently Fiona sensed you were growing tired of Margot and looking for a replacement.'

His snort of disgust was music to Lisa's ears. 'And you'll be glad to know Fiona wants us to be chums. In fact, she said I was almost as good as she at snagging a man, and she bears me no ill will. Mainly because she has hooked your father, and the money is all in the family.'

'It's no more than I expected from her,' Alex declared.

'Yes, well, I have often been mistaken for a bimbo, but if she were blonde Fiona would certainly take first prize. She quite happily admitted she doesn't love Leo, but his money.' Saying it out loud, Lisa couldn't keep her own personal sense of outrage out of her voice.

'Lisa.' He caught her wrist, his thumb idly stroking up her palm. She gave him a stormy look, and tried to pull her hand free. He smiled wryly and let go of her hand, but slid his arm around her waist, pulling her against his length. 'Forget Fiona. I will make sure she never bothers you. Now let's go to bed.'

Lisa's teeth ground together in frustration; her blue eyes flashed with temper. She did not want to go to bed, in fact she hated the idea, but she really had no choice. She supposed she should be thankful he had swallowed the reason for her anger without digging deeper, but she didn't feel grateful, just trapped. 'I suppose so,' she muttered.

Gleaming black eyes held hers and he laughed softly as though he knew exactly what was going through her mind. 'You're very young, Lisa. You still see everything in black and white. Unfortunately, life teaches one there are a dozen shades of grey in between. Don't worry about Leo; he knows exactly what he is paying for,' he assured her with cynical amusement.

She shrugged out of his embrace. 'I'm not that young, and I don't find it in the least amusing, and I bet your mother didn't either, the first time it happened.'

Alex winced. Her barb had hit home. 'All right.' He held his hands up in a gesture of surrender. 'I will say no more. Run along to bed. You've just reminded me, I have a call to make. My mother has to be told before Leo's latest escapade appears in the press.'

Lisa did not hesitate; she spun on her heel and headed for the dressing room.

Quickly selecting a plain white cotton tee shirt, she shot into the bathroom and stripped off her clothes. She completed her bedtime ritual in five minutes flat and walked into the adjoining bedroom. She stopped and stared at the huge bed and a vivid image of Margot standing in the exact same spot last night filled her mind.

It was no good; she could not get into bed with Alex and pretend nothing had happened. She simply could not do it. Turning, she headed for the door.

'I need a shower and shave, but I won't be long.' Alex strolled in from the dressing room, casually rubbing his jaw with his hand.

Lisa stopped at the sound of his voice and glanced at him, her eyes widening on his virtually naked body. Hot colour flooded her cheeks and she was helpless to look away. He was all tanned satin skin, sheathing rippling, hard-packed muscle and sinew, with a smattering of curling black body hair arrowing down over his flat belly to disappear beneath the band of a pair of black briefs that enhanced his masculine attributes rather than concealed them. She breathed in deeply and looked up, her wide blue eyes meeting deep brown.

In one lithe stride he was at her side. 'Why the blush? I am covered, and you have seen me naked before,' he teased.

'Yes, me and countless other women, I'm sure,' she snapped, brushing past him.

'Not so fast.' Alex's hand curved around her arm in a grip of steel. 'Now what is eating you?' he demanded, his eyes narrowing angrily on her furious face.

'Nothing, nothing at all. But I am not sleeping in that bed with you,' she told him bluntly. 'I suddenly realised there is not room on your bedpost for another notch, and I have no intention of being one of the multitude again,' she said with biting sarcasm.

'For heaven's sake, Lisa, it is only a bed.'

'Yes, I can see that, but somehow I had this weird idea the marital bed was something special. You, on the other hand, have shared that one with so many women I doubt you even know the score.' To her intense satisfaction she saw a dull tide of red darken his chiselled features. She realised she had actually managed to get through his arrogant exterior and embarrass him.

'You are far too sensitive for your own good,' Alex snapped, and, dropping her hand, he continued, 'But I take your point. Though for your information I can keep count, and it is nowhere near as many as you imagine.'

'That's the problem, I don't have to imagine,' Lisa responded, her eyes blazing up at him in hurt and anger.

'It's one thing to know your husband has had lovers in the past, but it's quite another to be presented with one of them naked, and by your bed.

'Our bed, Lisa,' he replied with silken emphasis. 'Margot and her ilk belong in the past. Accept it.'

His arrogant command made her blood boil. 'As Margot had to,' she sneered. Why she was defending the other woman, she had no idea, but he made her so mad. 'That woman loved you; I could see it in her eyes.'

'Love.' Alex lifted a shoulder in an infinitesimal shrug. 'Whatever that means, it was not something Margot was ever afflicted with.' His dark eyes mocked her. 'Now money, yes.'

A chill ran over Lisa's flesh and extinguished her anger at a stroke. She felt curiously calm. 'You don't believe in love,' she said softly, the effect of his *'Whatever that means'* slicing at the very heart of her.

Alex snorted in disgust. 'With a father like mine, what do you think?' he drawled. 'The man falls in love at the drop of a hat, or maybe the drop of a dress would be more appropriate.' His harsh laugh sounded the death knell of Lisa's hope. 'He compounds his stupidity by marrying them. Substitute sex for love, then you'll be nearer the truth.'

Appalled, she stood glued to the spot. Alex meant what he said; he really did not believe in love. It was several seconds before she could speak. 'Why did you marry me, Alex?' she asked quietly, her blue eyes holding his.

Apparently surprised, he raised his eyebrows sharply above his dark eyes, and, catching her by the shoulders, he drew her against him. 'I married you, Lisa, because I wanted you on sight.' He lifted a strong brown hand and let his fingertip trace the bow of her top lip in a fleeting gesture that made her body tense. 'After spending only one day with you I knew I had to have you. You are all I ever wanted in a wife,' he said softly, his dark eyes smiling into hers. 'Believe me.'

If his words were meant to reassure her, they failed miserably. Something deep down in Lisa shrivelled up under his charming smile. He didn't even realise his answer was an insult, she recognised sadly. Shrugging her shoulder free of his hand, she stepped back. 'Why me, and not Margot?' she asked quietly.

'Really, Lisa.' His dark gaze scanned over her stiff figure, a frown pleating his brow. 'You are not that naive. Margot is an actress.' He said it as if he was talking to a child, the exasperation in his tone clearly evident.

She shook her head in disbelief. The arrogant conceit of the man was absolutely unbelievable, and, raising her eyes to his, she prompted. 'Well, I'm a working girl.' She could not let it go. She was so vulnerable where he was concerned, loving him as she did. She had to know the worst, then maybe she could begin to get over him.

'Don't be so obtuse.' His deep brown eyes clashed with her brilliant blue ones. 'There is a world of difference between a thirty-something ambitious actress, and an intelligent, pure young woman who works and is protected by her family.' Alex's sensual mouth slanted sardonically. 'The first is strictly mistress material, and you, my darling Lisa, are the type men marry.'

'I see,' Lisa murmured, and closed her eyes for a second, fighting back the tears. She had fallen in love with a man who did not believe in the emotion.

'No, you don't see.' His voice tickled her ear and her eyes flew open. Alex had moved, and she stiffened as he slid a large hand around her waist and pulled her in to the hard heat of him. 'I married you because I was desperate with wanting you. No woman has ever affected me the way you do. And, much to my delight, I have discovered you have an endless capacity for enjoyment that perfectly matches my own,' he opined huskily. Lisa shivered as he pressed his lips to the pulse beating frantically in her throat. 'Now, let's go to bed, hmm.'

Afterwards, she would decide it was the softly drawled 'hmm' that had finally caused her to flip her lid...

Lisa curled her fingers into a fist, and swung with all her might, catching Alex a glancing blow on the side of his head. His arm fell from her waist and she turned on him like a mad thing. 'You have the most enormous ego of any man in the world, and you are deaf to boot,' she snarled.

Alex's hand came down on her slender shoulders and held her slightly away from him. 'What the hell was that for?' he demanded harshly.

'I am not sleeping with you in that bed. Got it?' she yelled. How he had dared to suggest it after what he had just revealed beggared belief.

'Enough!' Alex held up his hands, setting her free. 'Sleep in the guest room tonight, if you must. I will have the bed replaced tomorrow.' And with a last grim look at her red, furious face, he strode across the room into the bathroom.

Lisa slipped into the room she had occupied the night before and climbed into bed. She was exhausted, but the thoughts crowding her mind would not let her sleep. For a deliriously happy bride returning from her honeymoon only a few short days ago, confident in herself and the love of her husband, the past two days seemed like a horror story. But they were all too real and she had to face up to reality. Alex had his own reason for marrying her and it was not love.

Alex had taught her a hard lesson. To show one's innermost feelings with total honesty was damaging to one's health. Her marriage was over before it had really begun, though it broke her heart to have to admit it. She remembered all the times they had made love and she had spilled her heart out to him, declaring her undying love; it had never once occurred to her that Alex did not feel the same. More fool her...

She turned restlessly on the bed. Being brutally honest with herself, she admitted, it seemed huge and empty without Alex to share it with her. But she was not going to give in, she vowed. Alex had blackmailed her into staying with him. He had said his earlier threat to keep her with him had been a joke, but she was not so sure. She didn't know what to believe any more. All she knew for certain was she must keep Alex sweet until she found out exactly what he was up to with regard to Lawson's.

With her mind made up, she tried to sleep, but it was no good, she was wide awake. Slipping out of bed, she crossed over to her computer and switched it on. She had never felt so alone in her whole life, but blinking back the tears, she refused to cry. She E-mailed Jed. She needed to talk to someone, and the lonely hours before dawn in England were late evening in Montana; he might be on-line.

To her relief he was there. Within a very short space of time, Lisa was confiding to Jed the whole sorry story of her hasty marriage.

Jed listened and consoled, and his advice was optimistic. He pointed out she had not given the marriage much of a chance. Alex probably did love her, but was not capable of saying the words. She did not know for sure that he meant to take over her company. Why didn't she ask him? There might be a simple explanation. Anyway, she was his wife and was entitled to half of everything he owned. So was she being totally reasonable?

She replied. Was he simply sticking up for his own sex? Jed denied the accusation and reminded her she had been married in church, before God, and her vows were not something to dismiss lightly. They chatted for over an hour and Lisa, completely absorbed in what she was doing, didn't see the bedroom door open, or the tall dark figure of the man watching her. Nor did she see the tenderness in the gleaming black eyes that lingered on her slender body crouched over the machine…

CHAPTER SIX

ALEX manoeuvred his red Ferrari between two massive stone pillars crowned by Lions, past open gates, and gunned the car up a long winding drive.

'Are you sure this is the right house?' Lisa queried irritably. She had overslept this morning, mainly because it had been five in the morning before she had got to sleep. Alex had awakened her with a cup of coffee, looking disgustingly fit in blue jeans and a blue knit polo shirt, ready to go. She had forgotten all about their house-hunting and, glancing at him now, in the close confines of the sports car, she wished he had done the same. But no such luck. Alex pursued everything with a ruthless determination that was impossible to ignore.

Within half an hour of waking up Lisa had washed and dressed in white pleated trousers with a white and blue cropped top to match. She'd grabbed a piece of toast and had only taken one bite before Alex had marched into the kitchen. 'Mrs Blaydon, I have ordered a new bed for the master bedroom. Someone will ring and tell you what time it is arriving. Be here.' And, grasping Lisa's free hand, he had hurried her out of the apartment and into the car.

Alex's voice broke into her troubled thoughts. 'Of course I am sure. I am a brilliant navigator.' His dark eyes flicked her a smiling glance.

The car had breasted the top of a hill, and fifty yards on was the most impressive Georgian mansion Lisa had ever seen.

Alex stopped the car at the foot of stone steps that led to the entrance door, and turned to Lisa. 'You, my darling, should have eaten some breakfast, it might have improved your disposition,' he opined mockingly.

'And whose fault was that?' she prompted. 'You dragged me out of the apartment like you were taking a dog for a walk.'

Alex burst out laughing, his white teeth flashing 'You're certainly no dog!' His gleaming gaze slid over her mutinous face with genuine amusement, dropping to the proud thrust of her breasts against the soft cotton of her top, the slight glimpse of tanned midriff, and came back to her face. 'Though you have been acting like a dog in the manger for the past couple of days.' His dark eyes studied her intently for a long moment. 'I presume it is simply the effect of your period?' he asked quietly.

Lisa felt his intimate glance like a caress, and she trembled inside, but it was what he was *not* saying that worried her. A cynical angry Alex she could handle, but a questioning, analytical Alex was far too dangerous. *She* was trying to discover what deviousness *he* was up to, not the other way around. So she responded carefully, 'Yes, probably.' She managed a rueful smile. 'Sorry.' She had to get her act together and try to behave normally around him.

He leaned forward, his lips hovering within inches of hers. 'You're forgiven.' And he kissed her softly. The warmth of his breath brushed her cheek as he straightened up. She inhaled his clean, masculine scent and knew she would remember it to her dying day. Whatever happened between them.

'Come on, Lisa,' Alex commanded as he climbed out of the car. 'I want your opinion on Stoneborough Manor.'

Lisa slid out of the low seat and followed Alex to the

stone steps, squinting her eyes slightly to look up at the house. At the same time she smoothed her pants down over her hips, then tugged at her cotton top. 'It's a bit big.'

'The house, maybe. But that top is a bit small.' Alex grunted, eyeing the band of bare flesh between her top and pants, and the tantalising indent of her belly button.

'It's perfect for summer. You must be getting old,' she quipped with a grin. 'And you have to admit, it is a glorious summer day.' Weather-wise, at least, she thought privately. In every other respect she wished she was anywhere else than looking over prospective houses with Alex. Jed had tried to convince her to give her marriage a chance, but she was not so sure…

She had not changed her mind an hour later, after wandering around the magnificent Georgian mansion. It was the ideal family home. The interior had been tastefully restored and decorated quite recently. A large elegant hall, with a polished hardwood floor and a magnificent staircase as its centre point, made an immediate impression. The study and five reception rooms were equally as impressive, from the formal dining room to the drawing room, library, and the cosier sitting room at the rear, that opened out into a marvellous conservatory.

Six bedrooms, all with *ensuite* bathrooms took up the first floor. The attic had been converted into an apartment for staff. The master suite was a triumph in interior design. The huge bedroom was dominated by an elegant but massive four-poster bed. A door on one side of the room led to a small sitting room. On the other side, there were his and her bathrooms, and a dressing room. Whoever owned the house had spared no expense; that much was obvious to Lisa's admiring gaze as she walked across the deep-pile carpet and stood at the tall window, staring out at the view. It was breathtaking, like a secret valley, she thought fancifully.

Suddenly Alex's arms slipped around her waist, and the shock of his touch made her jump. She was keenly aware of his casual embrace, of his hands locked across her bare midriff, of his long legs pressing against her thighs, the way their bodies fitted together so naturally. His dark head bent forward, his cheek brushed against her hair, and she could not prevent the trembling in her limbs.

'What do you think?' he prompted softly.

'I think it must cost a fortune. And even more to furnish,' Lisa said jerkily, intensely aware of his powerful body enfolding her and reminding her they were alone in the house. Alex evoked a mixture of hate and love inside her in equal measures, but in the intimacy of a bedroom designed for lovers it was the latter that was threatening her self-control.

Alex's hands tightened on the side of her waist and he spun her round. 'Never mind the price; and as it happens the furniture is included—a lot of it was made for the house.' Cool dark eyes scanned her wary face. 'Do you like it?'

The thought crossed Lisa's mind that he seemed to know a lot about the place. Personally she loved the house. It was perfect, from the magnificent swimming pool and hot tub at the rear of the building, to the more practical kitchen and utilities, and the five acres of beautifully sculptured garden that surrounded the house, with a paddock beyond. But she was not about to admit as much to Alex. Two days ago she would have flung her arms around his neck and begged him to buy it. Not now...

Her blue eyes guarded, she held his gaze. The betrayal of trust in a relationship, she realised sadly, was probably the worst crime, and she formed her answer accordingly. 'Yes, it is a nice house, but it is the first one we have viewed. I don't think we should rush into anything. It is rather a long way from my work, plus it's rather isolated.'

'Hardly isolated,' Alex drawled sarcastically, his hands dropping from her waist, much to her relief. 'Oxford is a mere fifteen minutes away, and it is barely an hour to Stratford-upon-Avon. I would have said it was in a great position, being almost mid-way between London and Lawson's. But—' he gave a slight shrug of his broad shoulders '—if it does not appeal to you, so be it.'

'I just feel we should wait,' she insisted, glancing cautiously from beneath lowered lashes, wondering how he would take her less than enthusiastic response.

'In that case, shall we go?' he slanted mockingly.

'Yes,' Lisa agreed, and preceded him down the stairs and out of the house. She glanced over the building as he locked the huge doors. It would make some lucky family a wonderful home.

During the drive back to London Alex revealed that he had to go to New York on Monday, for a few days, and asked her if she wished to accompany him. Lisa swallowed back a sigh of relief as she refused, with the genuine excuse that she had to go to the office on Monday to begin interviewing prospective candidates for Mary's job.

On their return to the apartment, Mrs Blaydon met them with the information that the new bed had been delivered, and she had left a meal prepared in the kitchen.

Alex glanced at Lisa, a devilish gleam in his eyes. 'Thank you, Mrs B. You can leave now. Lisa and I want to check out the new bed.'

Lisa blushed to the roots of her hair. 'What did you

have to say that for?' she demanded as the housekeeper left in a rush. 'You embarrassed the poor woman.'

'Mrs B was not the one who was embarrassed,' Alex came back in amusement as he studied her scarlet cheeks.

'Oh you're impossible!' she burst out. She had spent all day in his company and she felt as if she had been walking on eggshells. 'And I am not sharing the new bed. I want my own room,' she demanded furiously.

Brilliant dark eyes rested on her defiant face. 'No way, Lisa. This foolishness has gone on long enough. Now, get into the kitchen and see what Mrs B has left for dinner. I am starving.'

Flinching from his blunt statement, and furious at his ordering her into the kitchen, she wanted to slap him. Instead she marched off and set about warming the chicken, mushroom and herb casserole the housekeeper had left.

The meal was a silent affair; Lisa had not the heart to talk, and, picking up on her mood, Alex ate in brooding silence too. When she occasionally caught his eye, she quickly looked away.

Lisa felt the swirling currents of tension building, and finally she could stand it no longer. Pushing back her chair, she stood up. 'I have some work to do on my computer. If you will excuse me.' She spoke to somewhere over his left shoulder.

'So polite, Lisa,' Alex observed indolently, leaning back in his chair and studying her with half-closed eyes. 'Why now, I wonder? When we know each other so intimately.'

As if compelled, she glanced at his reclining form, and the tempo of her heartbeat increased. She met his narrowed gaze with reluctance, her eyes lingering on his high cheekbones and dropping to settle briefly on his mouth, which was a mistake. It wasn't fair; she only had to look at him and the tug of sexual awareness was instant.

'Yes, well, I tend to be that way,' she finally answered. More than anything she wanted to lash out at him, and demand to know why he was plotting against her with Nigel. But she didn't dare. Not yet. If what she suspected was true, she needed to form a plan to defeat him. The fact that she ached for him with every pore she was just going to have to learn to live with.

'I know exactly what you are,' Alex said softly, rising to his feet and moving around the table to stop in front of her. His hand reached forward and captured her chin, tilting it slightly so that he could examine her delicate features. 'You're a very passionate young woman who has suddenly realised the enormity of marriage after playing at it for a few weeks.' His smile was stunningly sensual and she almost groaned. 'And perhaps you are running a little scared. That I can understand. So, go to your computer *agape mou*.' The endearment rolled off his tongue.

Lisa felt the effect to her toes, and his fingers on her chin tightened momentarily. She stared dumbly up at him, noting the glint of what looked almost like tenderness behind his grin. Her shoulders tensed against the potent spell of the fierce sexual chemistry he exuded without even trying. He reached out to brush a stray tendril of hair from her brow. She shivered, and his hard lips thinned. 'Suddenly I frighten you, Lisa, and I don't know why. Care to tell me?' he queried silkily.

Lisa took a deep, steadying breath. 'You're imagining things, Alex.'

'If you say so.' His expression did not change, but she could sense his anger. 'I have work to do myself,' he said casually, but something hardened the depths of his eyes.

'However, do not make the mistake of thinking you can avoid our bedroom tonight. You have no excuse.'

There was no mistaking the silent warning in his gaze, and it took all Lisa's considerable control to reply lightly, 'As if I would, Alex.' and she even managed a chuckle. She was discovering she had quite a talent for acting, smiling on the outside when inside she wanted to rage at her arrogant husband.

'Good girl.' And before she knew what was happening his dark head swooped down and his mouth caught hers. Warmth coursed through her veins, and helplessly she opened her mouth to accept his kiss. When he finally raised his head she stared mutely up at him.

'See you later, in our bed.' Alex said, his chiselled mouth curving in a confident grin at her all-too-obvious surrender to his kiss.

As it happened, Lisa did not see him again that night. At midnight she crawled into bed, and the effect of the last forty-eight hours finally caught up with her. She went out like a light, and when she woke up in the morning the only hint that Alex had shared the bed was the indentation of his head on the empty pillow beside her.

Sunday was a repeat of Saturday; the only difference was that the house they viewed was on the outskirts of Banbury. Luckily for Lisa, this time she did not have to pretend uninterest in the property, because she hated it on sight. A huge, very new redbrick mansion, from the outside it reminded Lisa of a supermarket. It did have one saving grace: it was so horrific, Lisa found herself laughing with Alex over the various rooms. Consequently she managed to get through the evening without the tension that had marred the past two days. They watched a video of the latest blockbuster film, and when Lisa went to bed

Alex simply said he would join her in a while; he had a few calls to make.

Lisa closed the bathroom door behind her and crossed to the bed. She pulled back the covers, and climbed into bed, tugging down the bottom of her crisp white cotton nightshift, and closed her eyes. She felt the light brush of warm lips against her own and sighed; she was in that hazy period before sleep, and lazily she opened her eyes. A naked Alex was bending over the bed.

'What are you doing?' she asked stupidly.

'Hush, Lisa,' he murmured, lifting the coverlet and sliding in beside her. She edged back along the bed, but a long arm reached out and curled around her waist. 'I simply want to hold you.' Drawing her against his hard body, he covered her face with countless little kisses.

Her startled gaze met a pair of amused brown eyes. 'But...'

'Hush, I know,' He whispered with mocking humour, continuing to press kisses to her cheek, the curve of her ear. His fingers brushed the pulse at the base of her throat and she sighed. Her lips parted and finally his mouth claimed hers.

The trouble was he knew her too well. She was helpless to resist the tenderness of his embrace, the curling of his tongue against hers, the delicious pleasure as his hand trailed down to cup the underside of her breast. He had a magic touch, Lisa thought dreamily.

A second later he lifted his head, 'What on earth are you wearing?' he demanded with a chuckle.

With the dim glow of the bedside light illuminating the room, Lisa stared up into his shadowed face. She had succumbed to him so easily she was ashamed. His dark eyes smiled down into her own, deep and lazily humorous, and his hand lifted to trace the soft contours of her breasts again, over the soft cotton of her nightshift. She felt a needle-sharp quiver of delight pierce her body, and she burst out, 'Get off,' and brushed his hand away. 'This is a genuine Victorian antique I bought in Bath.'

His roar of laughter would have wakened the dead.

'You can laugh, but it was very expensive. I had to search…'

'Shh.' He brushed his thumb over her lips. 'I'm sure it is lovely.' She could hear the lingering trace of laughter in his voice. 'And I know you're not well. But later, when you know me better and you are not quite so shy, I will teach you ways to make love that know no boundaries, ways you've never dreamed of.'

His deeply evocative words made the heat flood through her body, even as she reminded herself he did not love her, it was only sex on his part.

'But not now,' Alex husked, noting the flush of embarrassment on her lovely face. Replacing his hand with his mouth, he nipped at her lips, and she opened her mouth in ready acceptance of his tender, possessive kiss. 'I simply want to kiss you goodnight,' he whispered against her lips. 'We have had our first argument as man and wife.' His lips trailed to her throat and he laved the pulse that beat frantically in her neck. 'It should not have happened.' He raised his head and brushed her lips briefly with his own. 'And we will never argue again.'

It was so Alex! So arrogant. *We will never argue again.* He said it as if it was a done deal, Lisa thought, a wry smile curving her mouth.

Alex's dark eyes narrowed on her face. 'What is so amusing?'

'You… ''We will never argue again.'' Some hope,' she jeered.

'You don't agree? But there is no reason to fight. To build a good marriage one must learn to compromise.'

'You sound like you are quoting from a marriage guidance book. Some people like to fight.' Alex being one of them, she privately thought.

'Rubbish. It's a ridiculous waste of energy.'

'Alex, are you arguing with me?' Lisa asked sweetly, and her smile broadened at the look of exasperation on his handsome face.

'You're a witch. Close your eyes and go to sleep before I change my mind and ravish you.' And with one hard kiss on her laughing mouth, he rolled over on to his back and hauled her into his side. With his free hand he switched off the bedside light.

In the darkness, curved into Alex's large body, the warmth and comfort of him enfolding her, Lisa closed her eyes, and within minutes was fast asleep.

It was *déjà vu*, she thought lazily, the brush of warm lips against her own. But the voice shouting, 'Wake up, woman,' was not. Her eyes flew open and rested on Alex. He was standing by the bed, shaved and dressed in an immaculate grey silk suit with a white shirt and conservative grey and blue striped tie, apparently ready to leave.

'What time is it?' she demanded, dragging herself up into a sitting position.

'Coffee time.' He indicated with a tilt of his dark head the bedside table, where a large cup of steaming coffee was standing. 'Also time I left for the airport.'

'Oh, well, thanks for the coffee. I have to get going myself. I said I would be in Stratford by ten.' Lisa tried for a light tone. Which was no mean feat, considering for the first time since their marriage, she had just spent the night very comfortably in Alex's arms without making love.

'It is not too late for you to change your mind, Lisa, and come with me to New York,' he offered casually. 'I could, at a pinch, put off going until tomorrow.'

Lisa looked at him carefully. She could not believe he had said it, and for a second she was tempted, but quickly she squashed the idea. 'No. No, really. I have far too much work to catch up on.'

'As you like.' He leant down and pressed a brief kiss on the top of her head. Lisa looked up in surprise.

'Try not to miss me too much,' he commanded, a gleam of mocking amusement glinting in the dark eyes above her own.

The trouble was, Lisa realised with a sinking heart, she would miss him. 'I won't have time,' she returned brightly, ignoring her innermost feelings.

His dark gaze sharpened on her cool face. 'Hopefully after this week your work will no longer be a problem. It is not that hard to hire a secretary. Or you could consider selling the company.'

Lisa glanced away from his penetrating gaze, the word *selling* echoing in her head, her worst suspicion confirmed. Her eyes fixed on the folds of the coverlet, an icy chill penetrating her heart. 'I have no intention of ever selling, and finding a secretary for Mary will be no problem, I can assure you.'

'I certainly hope so. I have no desire to have a part time wife,' Alex countered with devastating frankness, and left.

So now she knew. He had suggested she sell the company. Her fingers curved convulsively in the coverlet. How long before he put himself forward as a buyer, or suggested razing the factory to the ground? she wondered on a shaky breath. And what could she do about it when he did?

*   *   *

Turning the key in the drawer which held her mother's papers, Lisa found what she was looking for. The offer to buy had been made by Xela Properties with no mention of changing the business. She debated ringing them, but decided to display caution. She searched the Internet instead and found Xela Properties, only to discover to her horror that Solomos International was the parent company to it and a host of others. Starting in alphabetical order: Alexsol Cruises, Alomos Financial Services, and, of course, at the end, Xela Properties.

Switching off her computer, Lisa stared at the blank screen. In a way it was her own fault. She could have checked to see if Solomos International had a web page ages ago, but it had never occurred to her to do so. So much for her idea of a white knight helping her. It had been Alex who had tried to buy Lawson's out a year ago...

The telephone rang, and Mary answered it. She listened for a second, then covered the mouthpiece with her hand. 'It's for you, Lisa. Your husband.'

Reluctantly Lisa reached out to take the call. 'Alex. What are you calling for?' she asked calmly, when she really felt like shouting every obscenity she could think of at him. He had been planning for over a year to get control of Lawson's and destroy it!

'I was not aware I needed a reason to speak to my wife,' his deep voice echoed down the telephone.

Sarcastic, devious devil, Lisa thought furiously. 'Yes, well, I am rather busy, so unless it was something important...' She paused.

'Not really. I thought you might like to know I have arrived in New York.'

'Oh, yes, great. But I haven't time to talk; ring again some time.' And she clashed down the phone.

Lisa spent the rest of the day interviewing people for a job she was not sure was going to be available if Alex had his way…

Over dinner that evening with Harold, she was surprised when he had asked her quite seriously, 'You do love Alex, don't you, Lisa?' His cherubic face was rather grim.

'Of course I do.' She forced a smile. 'What makes you ask?'

'Well, your mother expected me to take care of you, and I just wanted to make sure you were happy.'

For an instant Lisa was tempted to confide in him her fears for the company. As long as Harold voted his shares with hers, there would be nothing to worry about. He loved her like a daughter, and he loved the company and his job. But Lisa knew his one weakness was his son, Nigel. If Nigel asked him to sell, he might agree.

'I miss her.' Harold sighed wearily.

Looking at his sad face, she hadn't the heart to trouble him. No! She had to solve the problem herself, and, rising to her feet, she walked around the table and pressed a swift kiss on the top of his head. 'I know you do, Harold, we both do. But life must go on.'

'Yes, yes, you're right.' he declared emphatically.

Lisa's eyebrows rose in surprise at the determination in his tone, and what looked like relief on his round face. 'Well, goodnight,' she murmured, and went upstairs to her old bedroom. But it was hours before she slept, and when she did she dreamed of Alex.

Tuesday was even worse. Mary reminded her. 'You're taking Mr Brown from Beaver Pine to lunch today.'

Lawson Designer Glass sublet two work units, which provided extra income for the business.

Lisa looked up from scanning the references of the girl

they were considering employing and smiled. 'Yes, I know. Keep your fingers crossed he renews his lease.'

Two hours later when Lisa returned to the office, her face was set in a worried frown. 'What happened to you?' Mary asked. 'You look like you lost a pound and found a penny.'

'I have. Mr Brown was very polite, but he is not renewing his lease. He's moving to bigger premises on the new industrial estate. He also let slip that Curly Cane is thinking of expanding elsewhere as well. I'm meeting Mr George, the boss, tomorrow for lunch. I can just see it now. Both leases run out at the end of July. Come August, the height of the tourist season, we'll be the only firm operating; two boarded-up premises will not make a very good impression on our customers.'

'No,' Mary murmured. 'But it shouldn't be too hard to find other tenants.'

Lisa hoped she was right. Picking up the references she had been reading before lunch, Lisa scanned them one more time. At the interview, Miss Clement had come across as perfect for the job. The woman's references were excellent, but Lisa was in a dilemma. Last week she had been all for leaving Mary in charge and looking forward to a long and happy life with her husband. Now she didn't trust her husband and she had an uneasy feeling she might not be able to hang on to the company.

'Mary, get in touch with Miss Clement.' She had to think positively, and, standing up, Lisa crossed to Mary's desk. 'Offer her the job.'

Then she called Mr Wilkinson, her lawyer. She was going to ask him to put in an offer for the Lee shares. She would find the money from somewhere. Unfortunately he was on holiday until Thursday. Lisa explained to his secretary what she wanted, and the woman promised to inform Mr Wilkinson as soon as he returned. Lisa could do no more.

Thankfully, the next day, her lunch with Mr George went well. He had looked into moving but had decided against it. He took the new lease she offered.

Lisa returned to the office in a much happier mood than the day before, and it improved even further when Mary said Miss Clement had agreed to start on Monday.

By Thursday, Lisa came back from a visit to her bank manager, with a loan agreed and a genuine smile on her face, to find Mary standing by her desk. 'Good, you're back. Wilkinson and Morgan just called. Mr Wilkinson said, would you call him back?'

Lisa grinned. Her problems would soon be over. Five minutes later, she carefully placed the telephone receiver on its rest, her face pale beneath her tan. She didn't see Mary's concerned look. Her whole vision was centred internally. Mr Wilkinson had called to tell her the Lee estate had sold their thirty-five per cent holding in Lawson's to Xela Properties. Apparently Mr Wilkinson had tried to get in touch with her to ask if she wanted to make an offer for the Lee shares, but she had been on her honeymoon and he hadn't been able to contact her. So had Alex been honeymooning, she thought bitterly but that hadn't stopped him buying them, the sneaky, conniving, lying bastard!

'Are you okay?' Mary's voice cut through her rage.

'Yes, yes, I'm fine.' But she wasn't. She wanted to scream her fury out loud. Instead, when the telephone rang on her desk, she picked it up and yelled, 'Yes, who is it?' It was Alex. His timing could not have been worse. 'What do you want?' Apart from my company, she felt like adding.

'Not a very lover-like greeting. I simply wondered if

there had been any developments at your end. Have you managed to find a replacement for your PA yet?'

Developments! What a nerve. He knew damn well what had happened. She wanted to confront him with his duplicity, but instead she simply replied, 'Yes everything is fine.' Her mind was made up—she would fight him every inch of the way. She might have fallen into his arms like a ripe plum, but no way was she going to allow Lawson Designer Glass to do the same...

'Good,' Alex said. 'I will be back in London tomorrow afternoon. Bert is meeting me at the airport, and I will see you at the apartment.'

'Right, goodbye.' She didn't trust herself to say more, and she replaced the phone with rather more force than was necessary. She glanced at Mary. 'I'm leaving now and I won't be in tomorrow.' She said, and walked out of the office, out of the building, and slid behind the wheel of her red BMW—her one indulgence—drove out of the car park and straight home.

On Friday afternoon, Lisa sat on the train to London, outwardly a beautiful, elegant young woman, but inside a mass of conflicting emotions. To say she felt mad was an understatement; she was blindingly furious! She had E-mailed Jed before she left home. But even his words of wisdom had not calmed the rage in her heart. He had advised to simply confront Alex and demand the truth. To explain to Alex that absolute honesty was a prerequisite for a good marriage. She had laughed out loud at Jed's message. How come a young man almost the same age as herself had more insight into relationships than the older, arrogant swine she had married?

By the time the train was pulling into the station Lisa had calmed down somewhat. She had done a lot of soul-searching last night, and had analysed her behaviour, and reached a conclusion. She had allowed herself to be completely overwhelmed and overawed by her husband. Probably because it had all happened so quickly, and because Alex was her first and only lover. Or maybe because he was older and she had not considered herself an equal partner in the marriage. Obviously neither had he. He had bought shares in her company without even telling her. But he wasn't getting away with it…

The train stopped and Lisa stood up. She had dressed carefully in a smart, double-breasted, button-through navy blue linen dress, its wide belt accentuating her narrow waist. She smoothed the skirt of her dress down over her hips and picked up her brief case and laptop before leaving the train. In minutes she was in the back of a black cab and heading for the penthouse. Alex Solomos had a lot of explaining to do. She was going to confront him, something she should have done a week ago.

Lisa fitted the key into the lock and pushed open the door, and walked into the apartment. She didn't know what time Alex was due back, but it was now four p.m., so he couldn't be much longer. She walked straight through to the inner hall and disposed of her briefcase and laptop in her so-called study and, turning, walked back out.

'A bit late, Lisa.' Alex's deep voice held a mocking edge, and she spun around as he strolled out of the master bedroom.

'You're back.' Her startled gaze focused on his tall, hard-muscled frame. He had obviously not long stepped out of the shower. Incongruously, on such a masculine man, a pink towel hung low on his hips; another was slung around his neck, and his black hair was ruffled and wet, as if he had just been rubbing it. Her mouth went dry. It had only been a week, but the familiar rush of awareness curled her stomach.

'Not quite the response I hoped for,' Alex revealed as he walked towards her.

'You surprised me,' Lisa got out. Her blue eyes clashed with his, and what she saw in their darkening depths sent a jolt of sexual excitement quivering along every nerve in her body. She couldn't move, and she watched mesmerised as he closed the distance between them.

'I surprise myself,' he murmured enigmatically, and, raising his hands, he closed them over either side of her head, his long fingers raking through her hair, sending pins flying in every direction.

'Don't.' She tried to shake her head but his dark head dipped and his mouth crushed down on hers, stopping the words in her throat as he ravished her mouth with deep, hungry passion that she was helpless to deny.

A tiny voice of reason told her she must stop him. Lisa reached out to push him away, but it had been so long. When her hands came into contact with his bare chest she felt him shudder, and that was her undoing…

CHAPTER SEVEN

FLAT on her back on the bed, the skirt of her dress bunched up around her hips, Lisa drew a shuddering breath and gazed up at Alex, looming over her. She glanced frantically round the room and wondered how on earth she had got there. A few minutes ago she had been in the hall. Her stunned gaze returned to Alex. His night-black eyes traced the long length of her bare legs to settle at the juncture of her thighs. 'Alex,' she gasped breathlessly, taken aback by the fierce sexual hunger in his burning gaze.

'Yes, Lisa,' he rasped harshly, casting aside the towel, magnificently uninhibited by his aroused state. Her heart began to pound, and, to her shame, her traitorous body responded instantly to his aggressive male virility. He leant over, his fingers fumbling with the buttons down the front of her dress. The belt frustrated him and he simply tore the front of her lace bra, freeing her breasts to his avid gaze, then he reached down, kneading the creamy softness of them with his hands. She could not disguise her need, and when one hand reached for her briefs, she instinctively raised her pelvis to help him whisk the scrap of lace from her body.

'I want you,' Alex admitted fiercely, coming down on the bed and curving strong hands around her hips. Nudging her legs apart, he eased his strong thighs into the feminine cradle of her hips, his awesome body trembling against her.

Lisa, reeling from the speed of his seduction, still might

have made some effort to protest. But his firm lips fell upon her mouth and he kissed her with such ferocious need all thought of denying him was wiped from her mind.

'I have to have you; I can't wait,' Alex declared in a deep growl, his dark head dropping to press his mouth to the slender curve of her throat, mouthing dark husky words in Greek against her tender skin with an eroticism that made her heart shake. He trailed one hand up over her thigh, expert fingers seeking the fold of tender flesh that masked her femininity. Lisa trembled, a fierce primeval heat racing like wild fire through her veins, consuming her mind and body.

'You want me. You are so ready,' Alex grated with satisfaction. His long fingers discovered the hot moist core of her, teasing and tormenting her ultra-sensitive flesh until she became a slave to the agonising pleasure his touch evoked.

'So sweet, so hot… You've been aching for this all week,' Alex murmured huskily, lowering his mouth to tease and lick her nipples with delicacy until they were hot, hard peaks. 'I know I have,' he mouthed against her silky skin.

Lisa twisted and squirmed against him, consumed by a desire so fierce it was almost painful. She clutched at his broad shoulder, her misty blue gaze clashing with his as he raised his head. She stared up into his handsome face and his dark eyes burned black with the effort he was making to control his passion, a question in their glittering depths.

'Yes, yes!' She pleaded for his possession, and relief from the primeval passion that consumed her. His mouth descended on hers, parting her lips with a hungry sensuality she more than matched. She cried out when he moved, his strong hands lifting her hips, and she felt him glide, hard and urgent, into the velvet heat of her body. Her whole being centred on Alex. She clung to his broad shoulders, her long legs wrapping around his waist as he forced himself deeper and deeper with each stroke. Her body met each thrust, the raw power of his possession filling her with spiralling desire, until the familiar fierce wild pleasure swamped her, and her whole body convulsed in frantic release. Alex reared back, the tanned skin pulled taut across his high cheekbones, his black eyes unfocused, as Lisa's inner muscles contracted around him, and with one final thrust his great body followed hers into a shattering climax.

She felt his full weight relax on her, but she did not care, languorous in the aftermath of total physical satiation. She stroked her hands softly up his broad back with feline delight. He was hers. The thought registered, and with it reality. He was not hers, never had been. His reasons for marrying her were varied, but love was not part of the equation. She dropped her hands to the bed, suddenly chilled.

Alex rolled off her, breathing hard, then as his breathing steadied he turned towards her, his head propped on one elbow, and contemplated her rosy face with a lazy smile playing around his sensuous mouth.

'Now that is what I call a homecoming,' he drawled. 'In every sense of the word.'

Immediately on the defensive, Lisa avoided his amused gaze and tugged at the bodice of her hopelessly crushed dress. 'You could have waited until I was undressed,' she said, smarting at the inelegant picture she must present and heaving a sigh of relief when she finally got the offending garment down over her hips.

'Such modesty.' He chuckled. 'But totally unnecessary.' And, skimming one hand down over her stomach, he followed the line of her hip and thigh, smoothing the fabric until he reached the hem. 'Here, let me help you.' On the pretext of straightening the top of her dress, his teasing fingers sneaked across her breast.

Lisa swallowed hard and hastily sat up. Flinging her legs over the side of the bed, she stood up. 'I need a shower,' she muttered, and dashed for the bathroom, Alex's husky laughter ringing in her ears.

Lisa dragged the remains of her clothes off and stepped into the shower stall. 'Damn you, Alex,' she mouthed as she turned on the shower tap and lifted her head to the powerful spray. Alex was back, and she could not believe how easily she had fallen into his arms. Where was the cool, sophisticated image she had decided to adopt? The cutting questions she had for him regarding her company? Gone the same way as her dress, she thought bitterly, crushed to bits by her inability to resist the potent sexuality of her husband. Sighing, Lisa closed her eyes and, shaking her head, allowed the water to soothe her turbulent emotions.

'Need any help?'

Lisa's eyes flew open and she spun round on the wet tiles. Only Alex's long tanned arm curling around her waist stopped her from slipping to the floor. 'No, I can manage,' she spluttered.

'But it is much more fun my way,' Alex pronounced. With the water cascading down over both of them, his eyes were dark, slumberous as they slowly traced over her slim curves. 'You are so perfect,' he whispered throatily, his hand lifting to cup the underside of one breast, his thumb delicately scraping over the pert tip. 'So responsive.'

The slow ache deep within her began to spread, rekindling a flame of desire so potent she had to bite her lip to stifle the groan that threatened to sound her surrender once again. It wasn't fair. No man should have this much power over her. Throwing back her head, her blue eyes clashed with brown. 'I want…' to talk, she had been going to say, but at that instant his other hand curved around her waist and, lifting her up, he swung her out of the shower.

She clasped his wide shoulders, his tanned skin wet and smooth as satin beneath her fingers. She trembled when her naked body brushed in intimate contact against his as he gently set her on her feet. She swallowed hard, shamed by her body's swift response. She lifted angry eyes to his impossibly handsome face, humiliated by the strength of her passion for the man.

'I know exactly what you want.' Alex slanted a brilliant smile of masculine satisfaction over her warm cheeks. 'The same thing I do,' he declared throatily, flicking a glance over the proud thrust of her breasts and back to her face.

It was the smile that did it. Shame was submerged by sheer, ungovernable rage and she told him the truth as she saw it. 'You have taken me for a fool long enough, Alex,' she breathed.

'I've taken you many times, but never as a fool.' Alex surveyed her with the disturbing light of amusement in his eyes.

Without even thinking about it, Lisa swung her hand and tried to hit him. Instead, shocked by the speed of his reaction, she found her wrist caught and her naked body pressed hard against him. 'No.' Alex controlled her easily with his superior strength. 'This has gone far enough. I explained about Margot, she is no longer an issue, but something else has been eating you since last Friday. I made allowances because of your condition, but you no longer have that excuse.' His black brows drew together in a frown. 'I want the truth. What supposed sin have I committed in your mixed-up female mind?'

His tall, muscular frame towered over her. She stared up into his black questioning eyes, her own wild with fury. 'I know you own Xela Properties.' Lisa planted her free hand on his chest to put space between them. This time she was not going to be seduced by his body, she vowed, adding scathingly, 'Need I say more?'

'So?' One dark brow arched sardonically. 'What's new about that?' He demanded, releasing her in a cool, almost careless manner. Catching a towelling robe from the back of the door, he slipped it on before handing her a matching one. 'What is your point?' he queried, his firm mouth quirking in amusement. 'Presuming you have one, that is.'

Lisa almost choked on his patronising words. She felt like screaming in frustration. Instead, she pulled on the plain white robe and fastened the belt firmly around her waist. He thought it was a joke. She probably was a joke to him—the naive innocent, to be used when and how he wished. Lisa curled her fingers tightly into her palms, fighting to control the rage boiling inside her. But she needed all her wits about her to confront Alex, because he had the uncanny ability to turn off his emotions with the flick of a switch.

'Well, I'm waiting. I suppose waiting in bed would be out of the question?' he said, a wicked gleam in his eyes.

She swept her wet hair back from her face. 'You've got that right,' she snarled, and with a defiant toss of her head she glared at him. What the hell? she thought. He might as well have the whole truth; he couldn't hurt her more than he already had. 'I know you were behind the offer to buy Lawson's long before we ever met.'

'An oversight on my part. If I had known, the first and only time I visited the site, that the owner's daughter was such a beauty, I would have insisted on meeting you,' he informed her with a sexy grin.

She couldn't believe the audacity of the man; he still thought it was funny. He really was a heartless beast and the anger drained out of her. 'Don't pretend, Alex. You know exactly what I mean. I do not appreciate being married for the property I own,' she said bitterly.

The amusement vanished from his eyes; his mouth hardened in a thin, ominous line. 'If that is what you really think, then perhaps it *is* time we talked.' Turning, he walked back into the bedroom.

Lisa had no choice but to follow him. He had stopped in the middle of the floor and now moved around to face her. She glanced at him, a tall, dark giant of a man with cool, remote eyes, and then quickly looked away. She saw the rumpled bed, her mouth twisting in disgust at the evidence of her own weakness where Alex was concerned. What was the point of talking? Alex hadn't denied marrying her in an attempt to gain control of the company. There was nothing more to say…

She half turned, but long tanned fingers closed over her shoulders and wheeled her back to face him.

'You can't throw out an accusation like that and walk away, Lisa.' His dark eyes raked over her hostile face. 'When I married you, the company you owned was the last thing on my mind.' His deep husky drawl feathered along her taut nerves as smooth as silk. 'And, if you remember, the first day I took you out I told you I was the owner of Solomos International and asked you if it would be a problem. You said no.'

'But you never told me you were Xela Properties.' Lisa snorted. 'A very sneaky omission on your part.'

'I naturally supposed you knew. It is all there on our web site, and with your love of computers I find it amazing you're now telling me you never bothered to check it out. Any businessman worth his salt, when presented with a buy-out, would naturally investigate the company making the offer,' he said with cool reasoning.

Lisa stared up at him, appalled. What he said was true, but at the time her mother had just been diagnosed as terminally ill. The offer had been refused and banished from their minds. But he was right, damn him! Yet she was still convinced that if he had really wanted her to know he would have come straight out and told her. 'Very plausible, but I don't believe you,' she countered with a disdainful shake of her head. 'I know everything.'

'Not everything.' His sensual mouth twisted in the shadow of a smile. 'You are so young, so impulsive, Lisa, but life is rarely black and white, as I have told you before.' His long fingers kneaded her shoulders.

But Lisa wasn't fooled. He used his powerful masculine sensuality as a weapon to control her. Call me an idiot, why don't you? she thought furiously, incensed anew by his superior, patronising air.

'Please spare me your platitudes. I know you have already bought thirty five per cent of the company. But understand this: I will do my damnedest to make sure that that is all you get.' Lisa let fly with all the pent-up fury of the last week. 'You disgust me. You are the most devious, despicable man I have ever had the misfortune to meet, and my sincerest wish is that I never have to set eyes on you again.' And with one great effort she pushed him away.

'Believe me, Lisa. I would never hurt you,' Alex said softly.

'Trying to take over my company is not supposed to

hurt?' She eyed him bitterly. In his own way, Alex probably saw nothing wrong in what he had done. He was a businessman first, last and always.

'I am not trying to take over anything. I have bought out the other shareholders, that is all,' he asserted.

'That is impossible.' She knew he had bought the Lee shares, but Harold's? Never! 'I don't believe you.' Her stormy blue eyes clashed with his. 'You're lying. Harold would never sell without consulting me.' She saw a flash of what looked like pity in his dark gaze, and a peculiar sense of foreboding rose up inside her.

'I'm sorry to disappoint you, Lisa. Andrew Scott, my London manager, completed the deal last Tuesday. But it was for your own good.'

Nothing was more calculated to stiffen Lisa's backbone than her most hated phrase in the English language: *For your own good.* Invariably, it meant the exact opposite. 'And how did you persuade Harold to betray me?' she asked flatly.

'I didn't have to; he loves you. Apparently you convinced him it was time to move on.'

With a rising sense of inevitability, she cleared her throat, determined to go down fighting. 'Now you're going to tell me it's for my own good that Lawson Designer Glass will be razed to the ground to make way for some poxy redevelopment,' she prompted sarcastically. 'Well, it won't work; I still have overall control.' She was lying, but she was banking on Alex not knowing that.

His firm mouth quirked at the corners. 'Actually you do not have a majority; the Hospice sold their shares yesterday.'

Shock held her rigid. Her anguished eyes roamed over his arrogant dark head. 'Oh, God!' Lisa exclaimed. Alex now owned fifty-three percent of Lawson's. He had done

it. Bought her company from under her. 'You really are
the devil! You used sex to blind me, while robbing me
blind.' How could she have fallen in love with a man so
lacking in any moral fibre? A man who had played on her
innocence of the male sex to manipulate her into marriage
and, cruellest of all, to rob her of her birthright. Easily,
she thought sadly. She had recognised the dark power of
his personality the moment she had met him. But love had
blinded her to the ruthlessness inherent in the man.

'I seem to recall, not so long ago, your body welcoming
mine with an eagerness you could not hide. Far from being the devil, I am your guardian angel,' Alex offered
tautly, his narrowed eyes colliding with hers. 'I bought
the shares so you could keep your company.'

A harsh laugh escaped her. 'Excuse me, but it was already mine,' she reminded him bitterly, ignoring his crack
about sex.

'If I had not bought the shares, somebody else would
have done.' Alex shrugged. 'Solomos International is an
incredibly wealthy company, Lisa. We invest in many and
varied projects all over the world. Do you really think it
matters to me if we have one more site?' he said, exasperation lacing his tone. 'In fact, I have decided to cut
back on my workload since meeting you.' He glanced at
her lovely proud face, and something very like compas-
sion moved in his dark eyes. 'I know it's not your fault
you ended up in the position you have, Lisa. Grief can do
funny things and make fools of us all. It was an admirable
gesture in memory of your mother to donate those shares,
but it did put your business in a vulnerable position.
You're an intelligent woman, but you are very young and
lack experience. Have you any idea how quickly you
would have been out on your ear if any other firm had
bought into your company?' Not waiting for an answer,

he added, 'You were a sitting duck when you made that gift to the hospice.'

'And you shot me down.' But it was slowly dawning on her that there was an awful lot of truth in what Alex said. Had she made a terrible mistake?

'The hell I did,' he said savagely, reaching out and grabbing her shoulders. 'I saved it for you.'

'Oh, so how do you work that out, pray?' she enquired sarcastically.

Alex's hands tightened for a moment on her shoulders, and then he released her, the expression on his handsome face bleak. 'Trust me, Lisa; you don't need to know.'

'But I don't trust you,' she said bluntly. 'Not any more.'

He stared hard at her for long, tense seconds, the line of his jaw taut. She thought she saw a flicker of something like pain in his black eyes, but she must have imagined it, because he turned and walked away, to stand looking out of the window. He came back round to face her. 'You'd better sit down; you are not going to like this,' he said curtly, and indicated the small satin-covered sofa that rested against the wall with a wave of his hand.

Her first thought was to refuse, but something in his expression made her hesitate to defy him. With a nervous tug on the belt of her robe, she crossed to the sofa and sat down. She tilted her chin, her eyes cold as they met his. 'So fire away. But try for the truth this time.'

His dark eyes flared briefly with anger at her slur on his honesty, and then he sighed. 'A year ago Xela Properties—one of my companies as you so rightly said— was approached by a broker with an investment opportunity. Lawson's Designer Glass was ripe to be taken over and the site developed more profitably.' He glanced down at Lisa. 'But then you know all this.'

'There was no mention of redevelopment in the offer my mother received,' Lisa snapped.

Alex simply arched one dark brow sardonically. 'No one shows all his cards to his opponent.'

Lisa frowned. Her mother had been dying at the time, and that made it somehow worse. She looked back at Alex; was he the sort of man to prey on a dying woman?

He read her mind. 'No. I did not know.' He began pacing the floor in front of her. 'Andy Scott investigated the feasibility of the deal, and approached me for permission to proceed, which, after visiting the site, I gave. The offer was turned down. The whole project was shelved and would have stayed that way.'

'And that was when you decided to use more devious means, like marrying the owner,' she cut in, hurting from the way he had tricked her.

'Don't be ridiculous, Lisa, I did not even know you then,' Alex snapped. 'And I could buy and sell your company a million times over. I certainly did not marry you to persuade you into parting with it.'

Put like that, it did make her fears seem a bit groundless, but it did not alter the fact she had overheard him plotting with Nigel. 'So you say,' she mumbled, still not prepared to believe him.

He stared down at her for a moment, his dark eyes cold and angry. Then he renewed his pacing. 'I walked into the bar of a hotel in Statford-upon-Avon and I saw a beautiful elegant blonde with legs to die for. Then I saw her two companions—older, shorter, fatter and dark—nothing like the girl. I concluded they must be her sugar daddies.'

Lisa gasped in outrage. 'You've got a nerve, especially with your record with women.' Then she remembered his dismissive glance at the time and realised why.

'Yes, cynical of me, I know, but true. Then Nigel, your

stepbrother, introduced himself to me, claiming Andy
Scott as mutual acquaintance. I'm sorry to have to be the
one to tell you, Lisa,' he said with unaccustomed gentle-
ness, 'but Nigel was the commercial property broker who
first brought Andy Scott's attention to Lawson Designer
Glass.'

'How could he?' Lisa whispered to herself. But, knowing Nigel, she believed it.

Alex heard her. 'Quite easily, I'm afraid. I know you
consider him family. But he couldn't wait to inform me I
was missing out on a great deal. He suggested I raise the
offer and it would be second time lucky. He could guarantee delivering Harold Watson's thirteen per cent—and
if I wasn't interested, he told me, he had another company
lined up that was. I wasn't particularly keen. The Lawson
family was still left with fifty-two per cent—not a very
viable proposition for Xela Properties.'

'But if that's true, if you really did think like that, why
did you go behind my back and buy the shares?' Lisa
asked quietly.

He stopped pacing and stood in front of her, a deep tide
of colour darkening his handsome face. 'Because Nigel
pointed you out on that night in Stratford as the owner
and was quite effusive about your…' he hesitated.
'…character, shall we say, and the relationship between
you. He suggested a man of my experience should have
no trouble talking you round.' He had the grace to look
ashamed for a second. 'I would like to think my intentions
were noble at the time. It was immediately apparent to
me that Nigel was a rogue. I could barely remember the
deal he was talking about. I had to ring Andy later that
night to refresh my memory. But, to be honest, at the time
I simply saw a beautiful girl, who was not the freeloader

I had first thought, and jumped at the chance of an introduction.'

Flattering though it was to be called beautiful, Lisa wasn't fooled, and, leaping to her feet, she cried, 'I was right all along. You and Nigel *are* in it together!' Spinning on her heel, she stormed past him.

'Stop.' His hand caught her arm and pulled her around. 'Don't you dare walk away from me.' His hard, angry eyes roamed over her face. 'You are going to hear me out, even if I have to pin you to the bed to do it. So make your choice.' Suddenly she was very conscious of his large tanned body. His robe hung open to the waist, revealing his broad hairy chest, and when she glanced up at his angry face he met her look with hard, mocking eyes.

'All right,' she muttered, and sat down on the sofa. But this time Alex sat down beside her.

He caught her hands in his. 'To prevent you lashing out,' he said grimly, 'I have had enough of your histrionics.'

He continued as if he had never stopped. 'When you agreed to marry me, your company was the last thing on my mind. But I did tell Andy Scott to keep a wary eye out for any developments, and also to watch Nigel Watson. I did not trust the man. You were shortly to be my wife, and I naturally wanted to protect your interests.'

'Don't you mean your own?' she sneered.

'No, damn it, I don't! The third day of our honeymoon I received a fax from Andy Scott. He had some disturbing news. Nigel had approached another property company with the proposed deal, and they were interested enough to put in a bid for the Lee shares. I instructed Andy to string Nigel along with the promise of a finder's fee, and put in a counter-bid for Lee's shares, whatever it cost. That only left Harold's. Then, last Thursday, Andy made the amazing discovery you had given some shares to the hospice. I had no choice but to buy them.'

'You could have told me straight away,' Lisa said fiercely. 'I could have bought the shares myself. But, no, you had to be in control. I am telling you now, I will fight you every inch of the way if you try to close Lawson's down.'

Alex shook his head, frustrated as well as angry. 'For heaven sake, Lisa, we were on our honeymoon. I would have to have been the most insensitive man on the planet to have worried you with business at such a time. And I do not want to close Lawson's down. I might wish it had never existed, the trouble it has caused,' he opined dryly, 'but in fact you should be thanking me for saving it.'

'You don't want to demolish the place?' she queried, lifting wary blue eyes to his.

'I still think in the long term redevelopment is the best way forward, but I am perfectly happy for you to run the business as you like. I bought the majority share simply to protect you. You're my wife, and if it suits you to work I won't deprive you of the privilege. I meant to tell you last weekend, after checking the state of affairs with Andy on Thursday. But with the fiascos that night and the rest of the weekend turned into somehow I never got round to it. Perhaps because whenever I look at you I forget everything but this.' Alex wrapped an arm around her shoulders and his dark head bent towards her.

'No!' Lisa put a restraining hand on his bare chest. 'I am not going to be diverted by sex. Not again,' she said, quickly appalled at her own weakness. 'You see, Alex, I know you are lying. I overheard you and Nigel last Thursday in this very apartment. I heard you telling him he could invest in your development.' She still burned at the memory, and the tone of her voice reflected her feelings. 'The slimy rat. And you're no better.'

'I thought you loved your stepbrother. You told me you did.' Alex jerked back, his arm falling from her shoulder, his voice hard and accusing.

'You've got to be joking.' Lisa stared at him in genuine astonishment. 'I can't stand the man. I wouldn't give him the time of day if it weren't for Harold, and the feeling is mutual. Ever since he made a pass at me when I was sixteen and I made my feelings plain.'

Alex sucked in a deep breath, his black eyes glittering with some fierce emotion. 'I wish I had known that last week; I would have flattened the bastard.' He shook his dark head in a gesture of utter disgust with himself, and, grasping her hands in his hands, he asked, 'Why did you not tell me last Thursday what you had overheard? Am I such an ogre you could not talk to me?'

She shrugged wearily. 'What difference does it make? I heard enough to know my husband and stepbrother were plotting behind my back.'

'Exactly what did you hear, Lisa? I need to know.' His voice was flat, devoid of any emotion, only the tightening of his hands on hers told her he was nowhere near as calm as he appeared.

She stared unwaveringly for a moment into his taut face. Her teeth worried at her bottom lip. She remembered every word, they were carved on her brain but she wasn't sure she wanted to tell him.

'Tell me, Lisa,' he prompted curtly.

'All right.' And with complete honesty she told him. 'I heard Nigel say that after three weeks with the ice amazon he didn't blame you spending a night on your own. Then he asked you if the delectable Margot knew you were in town.'

'It was Nigel who told Margot I was in town. She confessed as much before she left,' Alex said flatly, and Lisa
winced. She had misjudged him badly. 'But I did not want
to disillusion you about Nigel.' He laced his fingers with
hers, as if to give her some of his strength. 'Go on.'

'There was a comment about a computer nerd.' It was
Alex's turn to wince. 'Then he asked for your confirmation that the sale of Lawson's would go through. You
teased him about getting my shares for nothing. And finally you said Nigel would get what he wanted.'

'What I actually said, Lisa, was that he would get his…
And I did not mean it in a friendly way. But I was la-
bouring under the impression you loved him like a
brother, so I had to put up with him, while making sure
he did not harm you. I was stringing him along that night
because, thinking ahead, I realised if anything happened
to Harold, Nigel would end up with a share in your business. There was no way I wanted Nigel to have anything
to do with you, so I had to keep him sweet until I had
done a deal with Harold.'

'You still could have told me. I never thought Harold
would ever sell without consulting me first. Until you
came along.' She glared at him, but her heart wasn't in
it. What Alex said made sense.

'Blood is thicker than water, Lisa. Harold is always
going to be weak where his son is concerned, and I realised it that night when I spoke to Nigel. Suffice to say,
after Nigel left the apartment I had a long talk to Harold.'

'Yes, you said so at the time.' Lisa knew that was true.
Was it possible Alex was telling the truth and he really
was not the villain she had painted him?

'I believe I did. Just before you seduced me.' He
stopped, an arrested expression on his handsome face.
'Now I understand,' he declared, a sensual, reminiscent

smile lighting his brown eyes. 'Your sudden aggression in bed last week was more fury than a fever of passion?' he queried softly, lifting their joined hands to his mouth and kissing her fingers.

'Never mind that.' She wasn't going there for anything! 'What did you say to Harold to get him to sell his shares?'

'I promised to pay off Nigel's debts.'

'What!' Lisa exclaimed. 'Are you mad?' She pulled her hands free and eyed her husband with stunned disbelief.

'I am now,' Alex said with wry amusement. 'When I learn he laid a hand on you. But it is too late. It is done. Harold loves his son, and would do anything for him, though he is not entirely blind to Nigel's faults. Harold and I agreed that the money I paid him for his shares would go into a trust to give Nigel an income from the interest. But Nigel can't get his hands on the capital.'

'And you did this for me?' Lisa said, feeling her way through what felt like a minefield. 'You bought the Lee shares first, to protect the company from a hostile bid set up by Nigel?'

Alex gave her a considering look. 'No,' he said and, rising to his feet, he stared fixedly down at her.

'No? But—' She raised confused blue eyes to his, and suddenly she felt the strong grip of Alex's hands on her arms, pulling her up against his body.

'I bought the shares for you, and only you. I don't give a damn about Lawson's, except as it affects you. You're my wife, my partner, and if you had shown a little more trust in me, talked to me, you could have spared us both a lot of unpleasantness,' Alex declared, with a disturbing intensity in his voice that left Lisa in no doubt he was telling the truth.

'I'm sorry, but it's not that easy to trust a husband when you think he's plotting behind your back, and then you're

confronted in the apartment you share by an almost naked
ex-mistress all in the same night,' Lisa retorted dryly. She
believed his explanation; she had to. Alex was the majority stockholder now, whether she liked it or not, and
did that matter if he was prepared to let her run the company as she wished? More than that, she loved him, and
eventually she might persuade her cynical husband to fall
in love with her.

'Okay, so there were mistakes on both sides,' Alex conceded. 'Mine being I should not have brought you back
to this apartment in the first place. I know you don't like
it.'

Lisa had to smile. 'Oh I don't know.' Placing a hand
in the open vee of his robe, she felt his hot satin skin
beneath her fingers. 'I seem to remember our wedding
night was not that bad.' Rising up on her toes, she pressed
her lips to his; his arms tightened around her and he took
over the kiss with a passionate thoroughness that had her
melting in his arms.

Suddenly Alex pulled back, his hands falling from her
waist. 'No, Lisa, I am not going to give you the chance
again to accuse me of manipulating you with sex.'

'I wasn't going to,' she teased, suddenly feeling light-
hearted.

'Good, then get dressed. We are leaving. We have to
learn to communicate better and here is not the place to
do it. Too many bad memories,' Alex insisted.

'I'll send you an E-mail from my laptop. Is that communication enough for you? Though I do remember over-
hearing you tell Nigel something about your lap.'

Alex stiffened, and she watched with laughter in her
eyes as his brow furrowed and he tried to remember, then
he disconcerted her completely by roaring with laughter.
Sweeping her up in his arms, he carried her to the bed.

'You're right. Who needs to talk when we have this?' And, with a wolfish smile, he dropped her on the bed. Falling down beside her, he deftly eased her out of her robe, shed his own, and drew her in to the hard heat of him. Lisa trembled violently, and wondered how she had ever been dumb enough to even consider forgoing such pleasure.

A long time later she lay with her head resting on his broad chest.

'Are you okay?' Alex queried softly. She felt the vibration of his words against the wall of his chest.

'I'm speechless,' she sighed.

'I'm surprised,' Alex murmured. 'You are usually such a verbal lover.'

'Yes, well, for once I am struck dumb.' But she knew what he was getting at.

Before she would have cried out in the throes of passion and declared her love in gushing terms. Not any more... She had accepted his reason for buying the shares in her company the same way she had accepted the fact that Alex did not believe in love. She told herself she didn't care, that the pleasure she found in his arms was enough...

'Good.' He rolled her on to her back and, propping his head on one elbow, he grinned down at her. 'How about a long weekend in Kos? Or perhaps you would prefer house-hunting again?' he ended less than enthusiastically.

Lisa pretended to consider. 'Well, a house is important...' She saw the flash of disappointment in his dark eyes. It was time to take a chance, and her lips parted in a purely feminine smile. 'But I doubt we'd find anything better than the first one we saw last week. So Kos it is.'

'You little witch.' Alex surveyed her with a disturbing light of understanding in his dark. 'You wanted the house, but you had so little trust in me you could not admit it, hmm.'

'Something like that,' she agreed.

'Hardly flattering, but understandable, I suppose.' Slipping off the bed, Alex picked up his robe and put it on. 'I have a few calls to make, so why not get up and get packed?' He glanced down at where she lay on the bed, her blonde hair spread in a tangled mass over the pillow, her body relaxed in the aftermath of passion, and his firm lips curved back over his brilliant white teeth in a blatantly sexy grin. 'And hurry, wife, or I might just change my mind!'

CHAPTER EIGHT

THE flight from London took a little over three hours and, allowing for the time difference, it was midnight when the jet touched down at Kos airport. They had travelled in the Solomos company jet, Alex explaining his father had been using it at the time of their wedding.

'Are you sure your mother won't mind our arriving in the middle of the night?' Lisa asked Alex, as he helped her onto the Tarmac.

Alex gave her a surprised glance and tucked her hand under his arm. 'You don't know much about Greek custom if you think midnight is late. In my mother's house we do not dine before ten, and quite often later.'

Two cars drew alongside them. In minutes, passport and customs details were accomplished, and Alex was ushering Lisa into the back seat of the second car, a chauffeur-driven limousine, and sliding in beside her.

'You must be famous?' She prompted. 'Not for you the queue at Customs!' She slanted him a sidelong glance. Dressed casually in jeans and a short-sleeved white shirt, he looked totally relaxed.

'Famous no, but local, yes. The population of the island is only twenty-five thousand, and most people here know each other. Actually, I had forgotten the first weekend in July is one of the busiest of the year. For the next two months the island will be heaving with tourists and the population swells to more like a million. For which I should be grateful.'

'Why?' Lisa tipped her head back to look up at him, intrigued.

'Because my father came here on holiday, met and married my mother, an island girl, and for the next few years built many of the hotels and apartments. In fact—' he looked down at her warily '—we are in the process of constructing a large holiday complex at the other end of the island, beside Paradise Beach. I thought I might take a look at it while we are here, see how it is going.'

'I might have guessed, you con-man,' she mocked. 'This is no holiday, but a business trip.'

'And who slipped their laptop in the side pocket of their holdall?' He asked drolly.

'Force of habit.' Lisa grinned at being caught out.

His dark eyes gleamed appreciatively down at her. She was a vision of loveliness, her blonde hair loose and curling around her bare shoulders. Her dress was a simple pale cream sheath in knitted cotton, the strapless bodice moulding her high, full breasts like the hands of a lover, the skirt ending a few inches above her knees. She had no idea how desirable she looked. Alex bent and placed a swift, hard kiss on her parted lips. 'So was that,' he said huskily.

At one in the morning, sitting on the terrace of the villa, sharing a soft-cushioned sofa with Alex and content in the curve of his arm, Lisa sighed blissfully. With the warm night air caressing her skin, the blue-black sky showered with sparkling stars above, and below, in the distance, the brilliantly lit shoreline and the sea beyond, she had rarely felt so relaxed.

'If you two young ones don't mind, I will say goodnight. I am so glad you are here, but at my age I need my beauty sleep.'

'So do we, Mamma.' Alex grinned and, rising to his

feet, took Lisa with him. Without releasing her he bent and kissed his mother's cheek. 'Goodnight.'

'Your mother is a lovely lady; I'm surprised Leo ever left her,' Lisa murmured as they watched the older woman enter the house.

'He didn't; she threw him out,' Alex said bluntly.

'Well, I can't say I blame her from what I've heard and seen of Leo. He can't keep his hands off women.'

'Life is never that cut and dried, Lisa,' Alex remarked, and, placing his other arm around her, he linked his hands lightly at her back. 'Women have a tendency to jump to conclusions, as you know,' he mocked her lightly, but the expression in his brown eyes was strangely reflective. 'I suppose nowadays medical science would have solved my parents' problem, but on an island like this thirty-five years ago, postnatal depression wasn't always recognised.'

'All the more reason for your father to stand by her, if she was ill,' Lisa argued.

Alex sighed. 'That is how I thought until a few years ago, when I had a fight with my father about his third divorce, and what it was costing, and he told me his side of the story. I don't condone his behaviour, but I do feel sorry for him.'

'I wouldn't,' Lisa murmured.

'No, but then you are not a man, thank God!' He gave her a quick squeeze that set her heart beating a little faster before continuing. 'Apparently, for two years after I was born, my mother would not let him anywhere near her. He loved her quite desperately and he was nearly out of his mind. He went to Athens on a construction project and while he was there my mother finally got over her depression. For the first time in her life she travelled to Athens by herself. Unfortunately, when she got to my father's hotel, he wasn't in. She waited in the foyer and saw him return, drunk and with a lady in tow. He swears it was the first time he had ever picked up a girl. I am inclined to believe him. My mother wasn't. She confronted him, threw her wedding ring at him, and got the next boat back to Kos. She has never left this island since.' Alex let go of her and, turning abruptly, caught her hand in his. 'End of story. Time for bed.'

She cast a sidelong glance at his harsh face as they walked into the house. 'And she never forgave him?' Lisa asked.

'No. One betrayal was one too many in her book.'

Lisa wondered if the same applied to Alex. In character was he like his mother or his father? She didn't know. But for her own sake she hoped it was the former.

Walking upstairs with her hand in his, Lisa wondered how Alex had felt as a small boy about the break-up of his parents' marriage.

They had reached the door of his bedroom suite, and, opening the door, Alex curved an arm around her shoulders and drew her inside, closing the door behind them.

She looked around the comfortable sitting room, and, suddenly nervous, she slipped from under his arms and walked out on to the balcony that ran the length of the building. 'It's hot.'

She felt Alex's hands close around her waist and his breath stir her hair. 'And it's going to get a lot hotter,' he husked. Awareness flared as his hands moved up to cup her breasts. 'This dress has tormented me all night.'

The breath caught in the back of her throat as he reached for the zip fastening and freed it. Lisa let her head fall back against him and made no protest as with deceptive ease he turned her to face him, the dress falling at her feet. Something vital leapt in his eyes and Lisa responded. Willingly she moved into his arms, and the kiss they shared was like no other. It was passionate, but tender, saying without words promises of hope, happiness, and need. Was it love? Lisa didn't know about Alex, but on her part it was, so why fight it?

'Bed, I think,' Alex opined huskily. His dark eyes gleamed down into hers. 'And I can guarantee no other woman but you has ever shared this bed.' Swinging her up in his arms, he carried her the short distance to the bedroom.

With an arm around his neck, her eyes level with his, Lisa's lips curved in a sympathetic smile. 'Poor Alex,' she mocked, 'would your mummy not let you?'

'Cheeky! But true.' And, sliding her slowly down the long length of his hard body, he let his hands drop to her hips, his fingers curling round the top of her briefs, her last remaining garment. He dropped to his knees on the floor, and with slow, delicate deliberation he slid her briefs down over her hips, at the same time covering her navel with his mouth. Lisa jerked and tried to pull back, but his hands would not let her. He pressed a kiss into the hollow of her hipbone She looked down and the trembling started in the pit of her stomach. Never had she seen anything so erotic as Alex's dark head against her thighs. He flicked a brief upward glance from beneath his thick lashes.

'I used to think I was a breast man,' he husked as he trailed his hands down the back of her thighs and followed with his mouth, pressing tiny kisses on her heated flesh. His hands continued their downward journey, curving her calves. 'But since meeting you, my sweet wife, I've decided I am a leg man.'

Lisa almost tumbled over when his hand lifted one foot, the trembling in her limbs was so great.

'Steady.' Alex chuckled as he helped her step out of her briefs. Slowly straightening up, a primitive glitter in his dark eyes, he let his hands sweep up her thighs and hips adding throatily, 'But then again...' his hands stroked up to her breasts '...your breasts are perfection.' His long fingers teased the sensitive peaks. 'I am spoilt for choice.'

Lisa groaned deep in her throat and focused on his darkly handsome face. She was shivering with excitement and involuntarily swayed towards him. He stopped her with the flat of his hand across her collarbone.

'No, Lisa, now it is your turn to undress me,' Alex declared roughly, but the fire in his dark eyes belied his apparent control.

Her heart thudding in her chest, Lisa raised her hands and slowly unfastened his shirt. She put both hands on his flat stomach and stroked up over his chest, her fingers tangling in his crisp curling body hair and grazing his taut male nipples. She eased the shirt off his broad shoulders, leaning forward to do so, deliberately brushing her breasts against his muscular chest. A secret smile curved her lips as she felt him shiver. It was an empowering feeling, knowing Alex was as susceptible as she was.

She let one hand drop to the fastening of his pants, and unclasped the top. Slipping her hand beneath the material, she was instantly aware of the strength of his arousal. Lisa glanced up at him through lowered lashes; his eyes were half closed, his lips pulled back across his teeth, and she had a daring idea. 'I'm not very good at this,' she said quietly, and turned guileless eyes up to his.

'I wouldn't say that,' Alex almost groaned. 'Go on.'

Her fingers finding the zipper, Lisa very slowly began to free it, pressing against his aroused flesh with her knuckles. 'I don't want to damage you,' she said breathlessly, and with both hands she slid his pants and briefs halfway over his hips and stopped. 'You're so powerful.' She edged one hand across his belly, her blue eyes gleaming with devilment and desire as they met his. Her fingers curved around him and gently squeezed, her thumb stroking the velvet tip.

Alex groaned for real. 'You little tease, Lisa.' And, pushing her hands away, he stripped off his pants in a second and tumbled her on to the bed. He caught her wrists above her head and, his lips, gentle as wild silk against her skin, trailed kisses over her eyelids, the soft curve of her cheek and finally her lips.

His tongue stroked the roof of her mouth, and then her own tongue curled around his in a welcome caress. Lisa ached to put her arms around him but he wouldn't let her.

'No, Lisa.' Alex raised his head; his night-black eyes met hers, a glint of mockery in their depths. 'Take turns— it's only fair.'

She arched against the hard heat of him as his lips blazed a trail of fire down her throat, lingering where the pulse beat wildly in her neck. Then he went lower, until his mouth closed over the tip of her breast.

'Alex.' She groaned his name as he suckled hungrily at her aching breasts, first one and then the other. Her skin tingled as if a million nerve-ends had suddenly come alive at his caress. 'Alex, please!'

He released her wrists and immediately she reached for him, her slender arms moving around his broad back. He captured her mouth again, and kissed her with an ever deepening hunger, and she kissed him back, one hand slipping around his neck, her fingers tangling in his hair to hold him to her, a fierce hunger, a need so great, exploding inside her. But Alex was not about to be rushed. With incredible control he led her to the brink of fulfilment over and over again. Soothing and enflaming her pliant body even as he fought to withstand her feverish intimate tactile exploration of his magnificent form. His strong features were taut and intent in passion, his black eyes flaring triumphant at her husky plea for release, and when she thought she could take no more he tipped her over the edge, and with a deep, rasping growl of release he followed her there.

Locked in his arms, his skin hot and damp against her own, Lisa stroked her hands lovingly over his shoulders and down his broad back. What did it matter if Alex didn't believe in love as long as they had this? He had shown her he wanted and needed her with a fierce and tender passion that touched her soul. Turning her head slightly, she pressed a soft kiss against the hard line of his jaw.

He eased his large frame to one side, and, leaning over her, he gently stroked a few strands of hair from her wet brow. 'All right?'

Her lips parted in a slow, wide smile. 'Never better.' She sighed, her brilliant blue eyes lingering on his darkly flushed face.

'Lisa, I…' Alex hesitated, his eyes widening on her delicate features almost in surprise. 'Meeting you was the luckiest day of my life,' he said huskily, and she had the distinct impression he had meant to say something else.

Midday Saturday, Lisa, hot and tired, gratefully took the hard hat off her head and handed it to Alex. Her hair was pulled back in a ponytail and she was wearing the minimum of clothing—brief white shorts and a sleeveless shirt knotted under her breasts—but still she had to wipe the perspiration from her brow. 'Do you visit all the construction sites your company is involved in?' she asked. 'It must take an awful lot of your time.'

'No.' Alex handed the hats to his site manager and said something in Greek, then, catching Lisa's hand in his, he added, as they walked off the building site, 'I employ a very efficient staff to do it for me. But as I was born here I do take a particular interest.' They had reached where he had parked the car and after opening the passenger door for her he walked around to the driver's side, and stopped when he saw she had not got in the car. 'Something wrong?' Not waiting for her answer, he tagged on, 'Sorry if you were bored.'

'Not bored. The view alone is incredible; the complex is bound to be a success.' She glanced at Alex. The blue cotton shirt fitted tautly across his broad shoulders, the first few buttons open to mid-chest. His black hair shone sleek as a raven's wing in the brilliant sun, and somehow, over the past few hours, he'd seemed more Greek to her than before. Looking at him, so cool while she was melting, she decided to get her own back.

'But you did promise we could go for a swim, Alex.' The maid had woken them that morning with a breakfast tray. She had set it on the table on the balcony and quickly withdrawn. They had made love for the fourth time. Then, when Lisa had been trying to get dressed, with a lot of interference from Alex, he had suggested she put her bikini on under her clothes and they could go for a swim later.

'So I did,' Alex drawled, a reminiscent smile curving his firm lips. 'But do you really want to join the tourists on the beach?' She eyed the wide sweep of Paradise Beach and the sparkling sea, a smile curving her generous mouth, her eyes gleaming with mischief as they met his over the top of the car. Sophisticated, arrogant Alex on Paradise Beach with hordes of tourists held great appeal. 'Yes, why not? It's so hot I'll melt.'

They spent the next half-hour playing like children in the warm clear waters, and then they dried off in the sun. Later still they returned to the villa and went to bed for a siesta, at Alex's instigation, insisting it was the Greek thing to do!

A sigh of pure pleasure left Lisa's lips as she sat down on a comfortable padded chair, one of two, set either side of a small table on the balcony of their suite and looked around her. Alex was downstairs talking with his mother. Apparently his mother had arranged a party for them to-night—a delayed wedding reception and a chance for Lisa to meet friends from his boyhood, she had said.

Lisa had left them talking and now, having showered and changed into a plain blue satin slip dress, she opened her laptop on the table in front of her and began composing an E-mail to send to Jed later. Enthusiastically she described the island, the history and the beauty of the place, and she smiled to herself when she thought of how green with envy Jed would be when he received it. Poor Jed had never been outside his state, let alone his country.

That was how Alex found her, smiling to herself, her fingers racing over the keys.

'Now who is working?' Alex prompted as he sat down opposite her, placing two glasses and a bottle of champagne on the table. 'And I was hoping to seduce you with champagne.'

'I wasn't working; I was writing to a friend,' she said simply, raising humorous eyes to his.

'A friend?' One dark brow arched quizzically.

'Yes, Jed.' She returned her attention to the keyboard. 'Usually I write down all the things I've been doing of interest. I compose my E-mail off-line and send it later, which is much more economical.' She didn't see the dark frown that creased his brow, or the slight narrowing of his deep brown eyes.

'Forget the economics.' Alex reached out a hand and brushed the back of her hand. 'Close that, and join me in a glass of champagne before the rabble arrive.'

'The rabble?' She grinned, closing her laptop. 'Not a very nice way to describe your friends, Alex.' She glanced across at him, struck by how vibrantly attractive he looked, wearing a cream open necked polo shirt and matching chinos, his handsome face tanned a deeper brown from a day spent in the sun.

'You haven't met them yet.' One brow lifted and his mouth twisted in an amused smile. 'Unlike your cerebral friends, mine are all too physical.' And, deftly popping the champagne cork, he filled two glasses and handed one to Lisa.

'That sounds ominous,' she replied, sipping the champagne.

His intense gaze caught and held hers, and for a second something hardened the depths of his eyes and she had the ridiculous notion she had angered him.

'Well, I will have to watch you like a hawk. No hardship in that dress,' he teased, allowing his dark gaze to skim across the soft curve of her breasts, revealed by the low neckline of her dress. 'Given half a chance they will throw you in the swimming pool, a favourite initiation rite, left over from boyhood.'

Alex was right about the party. It was a riotous affair. Yet Lisa couldn't help thinking that her arrogant, autocratic husband appeared much younger and much more open with his Greek friends than he had with the business friends they had met on their honeymoon. And she said so, when they finally got to bed at three in the morning. Alex's response was to laugh and to make love to her.

On Monday they left Kos. It had been a wonderful weekend, and Lisa watched through the aeroplane window as the island disappeared from view with a tinge of sadness.

'When do you think we'll come back?' she asked turning in her seat. Beside her Alex, immaculately dressed in a light suit and snowy white shirt, once more the consummate Greek tycoon, didn't hear her. His briefcase was open on his lap, his whole attention on the document he was reading. With a slight sigh Lisa returned to looking out of the window. Their dream weekend was well and truly over...

CHAPTER NINE

LISA signed off her computer and, with a contented sigh, sat up straight and stretched her slender arms above her head, easing the kinks out of her shoulders. That was her last job completed.

She glanced around the room, a soft smile playing around her full lips. It was hard to believe, but in the five weeks since they had returned from Kos Alex had bought the house at Stoneborough and three weeks ago they had moved in. Bert and Mrs Blaydon had accompanied them. A girl from the village had been hired to come in daily to help with the cleaning, and last Saturday they had had their first dinner guests.

Jake, who had been Alex's best man at their wedding, but who had vanished immediately after his speech, and his wife Tina had joined them for dinner. Apparently they lived a mere five miles away. Lisa had also discovered the reason Jake had exited the wedding reception so quickly. Tina had gone into labour that morning, but had insisted Jake could not let Alex down. Luckily Tina hadn't given birth until late in the evening, to a little girl, their second child.

Now, it seemed, they had a near perfect marriage, a beautiful home, a fantastic sex life. Alex made love to her until she didn't know if she was on her head or her heels. She drove to Stratford-upon-Avon and Lawson's one or two days a week, and the rest of the time she worked from home.

They could spend hours talking about books and music,

151

politics, even business. But for all that, Lisa felt beneath the surface of the relationship a certain tension, and she was incapable of doing anything about it. If she was honest she knew it was her own fault. But she could not forget Alex didn't believe in love. The fact that he seemed perfectly happy with their marriage simply added to her confusion, because she wanted it all.

Sighing at her own stupidity, she glanced at her watch. Almost nine; about time she thought about eating. Mrs Blaydon and Bert had gone to visit friends in London and were staying overnight, so she was alone in the house. Alex was in Singapore on business, and was due back tomorrow, Friday. Lisa couldn't wait to see him; she had missed him dreadfully.

She placed the cover on the computer's keyboard and reached to the printer, picking up the E-mail she had printed from Jed. It gave the address of the hotel he was staying in the following weekend. He was actually coming to London with a group of students from his college; they were on a guided tour of Europe: London, Paris, Madrid and Rome. Lisa had arranged to meet him at his hotel on the Saturday afternoon, the only time he was free. She was really looking forward to seeing the man who had been her confidant for so long. But she had never heard of his hotel, so she had taken the precaution of printing out the address. A taxi driver would have no problem.

'I thought I'd find you here.' Alex's deep melodious voice feathered along her nerves.

Lisa spun around on the swivel chair, the sheet of paper falling from her hand to the desk. 'I wasn't expecting you back until tomorrow.' She smiled, her blue eyes drinking in the sight of him. He was leaning against the doorframe, his tie pulled loose, his shirtsleeves rolled up to his elbows and the top three buttons of his shirt unfastened. He had discarded his jacket and his black hair was rumpled. He looked rakishly handsome and infinitely sexy…

'Yes…' He moved towards her and Lisa got to her feet, wishing she was wearing something more glamorous than an old pair of white Lycra shorts and a blue vest. 'I missed you, so I cut my visit short.' Alex's dark eyes swept over her slender body with a blatant sexuality that made her pulse beat heavily. His hands reached out to close over her shoulders. 'Dare I hope you missed me?' And he studied her face with a narrow-eyed intensity that for a moment arrested the smile on Lisa's lips.

'Of course I did,' she freely admitted. If only he knew how much! She wanted to fling her arms around him, but it wasn't necessary, as his dark head bent and his mouth captured hers. His strong arms encircling her, he kissed her with all the pent up passion of what seemed like years.

'I needed that,' Alex husked some minutes later, holding her loosely in his arms. 'I have had one hell of a trip. I need a shower.'

Aware of him with every nerve in her body, she let her luminous blue eyes roam over his darkly handsome face. He did look tired, and she ached with love for him. She linked her hands behind his head and pressed her face into the curve of his throat, nuzzling him with her mouth.

'Hmm, you do seem a bit ripe,' She commented, and with an exaggerated sniff lifted mischievous eyes to his.

'You will pay for that, woman.' Alex grinned, and, swinging her up in his arms, he carried her out of the study.

Later, after they had showered, they didn't bother to dress, but simply slipped on towelling robes. Lisa made a quick meal of scrambled eggs and tossed salad, and they washed it down with a glass of Chablis.

Seated next to Alex on one of the two comfortable sofas

in the conservatory, she looked out over the garden, and the trees beyond, and leant her head back against his shoulder, completely relaxed.

'You do like this house?' Alex asked idly, his breath stirring her hair.

She chuckled. 'Yes, Alex, I love it, and I also know you had every intention of buying it anyway because Tina told me you had viewed it the week before we were married.' Lisa had met Tina for lunch in the village pub on Monday, and had discovered quite a lot about her husband.

'For a tiny woman, Tina has a big mouth,' Alex said dryly.

'She also told me you play golf on a Saturday afternoon with Jake, whenever you are in England, and, surprise, surprise, the golf club you both patronise is two miles down the road.'

'All right. So you found me out. I am suitably chastised and, to show you the depth of my regret, I will take you shopping tomorrow.'

'Can't, I'm afraid.' Lisa turned her head and looked at him. I have a meeting tomorrow with a Mr Bob Burnett. Apparently he's a potter, and he wants to expand from selling to a few private galleries into leasing Lawson's unit and selling direct to the public.'

'What do you know about the man?' Alex asked, his hand slipping over her shoulder, his long fingers edging open her robe and then, seemingly idly, stroking the curve of her breast.

Lisa swallowed hard, her pulse quickening. 'Not a lot really, only the information Mary faxed me today: a copy of his application and a brief outline of his intentions. The fax is on my desk. I'll go and get it, and you see what you think.'

A gentle restraining arm tugged her back against the sofa. 'No, I'll go.' Alex stood up, his lips brushing the top of her head. 'You work too hard and I want you completely rested for later.' His dark eyes sparkled with amusement and a sensual promise that told her he knew exactly how he affected her.

A wide smile curved her generous mouth and she watched as he strolled out of the conservatory, her husband, her lover. With a deep sigh of contentment Lisa snuggled back against the soft cushions. Life could not be better. She was now totally convinced Alex had told her the truth about buying the shares for her protection. He had proved it in the last few weeks. Although he was the major shareholder, he took no active part in Lawson Designer Glass. He was quite happy for her to remain the boss. But he was perfectly prepared to listen and discuss any problems that arose. For Lisa, that was a pleasure which had been missing from her life since the death of her mother. To be able to discuss and debate her work with Alex was an added bonus to the intimate relationship they enjoyed.

She was a very lucky girl, and, curling her feet beneath her, she brushed her long hair, now almost dry, behind her ears. She couldn't believe she had actually thought of divorce a few weeks ago. She shivered. She had so nearly made a huge mistake, but then, didn't the cliché say that the first six months were the worst in a marriage? Lisa's eyes filled with latent laughter. In her case, it had been the first six weeks!

'Something amusing you, Lisa?' Alex's deep, melodious voice echoed in the silence.

She turned her head, her eyes unerringly finding his. He filled the conservatory with his presence and her heart did its familiar leap in her breast. 'No, I was just thinking. What took you so long?'

He lifted the fax in his hand. 'This. I read it.' He waved the paper in the air. Whether he thought it was good or bad, Lisa couldn't be sure. His dark face was curiously expressionless. Restlessly he prowled around the room, while Lisa watched him with lazy, loving eyes.

'And?' she prompted.

'I think your man appears to have been pottering at pottery, excuse the pun, using his garage as a studio. He needs that unit more than you need him,' Alex drawled cynically. He glanced down at her, his brown eyes assessing her sun-kissed features. 'Don't make a decision tomorrow. Have the man investigated first.'

'You have no faith in human nature,' Lisa teased.

Something bleak moved in the depths of his eyes, and then it was gone. 'I've lived a lot longer than you, Lisa. People are rarely what they seem.'

Her eyes held by his, Lisa shivered, suddenly chilled. 'Sorry, I forgot you're heading for your dotage,' she quipped, dismissing the shiver in her mind.

'Dotage, indeed! I'll have you know I am in my prime,' Alex informed her. He reached down and tilted her head back with one hand. His brown eyes darkened and she trembled in anticipation; she knew that look so well. 'Come to bed now, and I will show you,' he purred as he bent over her and his lips took hers in a long, lingering kiss.

The following afternoon, Lisa let herself into the house and dropped her briefcase on the hall table. The weather was scorching hot, and the drive back from Stratford-upon-Avon had been horrendous. She walked wearily upstairs to the bedroom, and kicking off her shoes, slipped out of her clothes. A shower or a swim in the pool? She couldn't decide. Grimacing, she walked into the bathroom and turned on the shower. Maybe her determination to keep on running Lawson's was not such a great idea. At the height of an exceptionally hot summer there was a lot to be said for being a lady of leisure. Especially with a husband like Alex.

Five minutes later, when Alex joined her in the shower, she almost told him as much. Except he diverted her very effectively from all normal thought by a gentle but thorough assault on her senses until she could only stare into his deep dark eyes, her own hazed with mindless desire. She hadn't even realised he was home…

Jake arrived midday Saturday, and whisked Alex off to play golf. Lisa spent a lazy couple of hours at the poolside before retiring to her study, and her E-mail, and that was where Alex found her on his return from golf.

'Talking to friends again?' he growled. 'I might have guessed.'

'You don't look very cheerful,' Lisa commented, swinging around to face him. 'Bad golf day? She arched one delicate brow enquiringly. He had a face like thunder.

'You could say that,' he muttered. 'I need a drink.' And walked out.

Lisa chuckled to herself. Tina had told her that Alex and Jake were fiercely competitive on the golf course, although they were the best of friends. Personally she couldn't see the fascination in knocking a little white ball around all afternoon. But it gave her some satisfaction to know her arrogant husband didn't win at everything.

The following Saturday Lisa glanced at the bedside clock and, pushing Alex's arm from around her waist rolled off the bed. 'Jake will be here in an hour for you, and I'm going up to Town.' She glanced back at his reclining form and caught a look of such terrifying anger in his eyes that she stopped. 'Alex?' she queried uncertainly. Surely he wasn't upset because she had got out of bed? They had made love already this morning, and last night. In fact for the past week Alex had made love to her every night and morning with a hungry intensity, a driven passion, that if she had not loved him so much she might have found disturbing.

'Lisa?' he mocked, one dark brow arching sardonically. 'I understand; less than three months and our honeymoon is definitely over.' And rolling off the other side of the bed, he stood up. 'I am collecting Jake today. So I'd better get a move on.'

Reassured, Lisa blew him a kiss from her open palm, and, turning with a deliberate wiggle of her hips, she sauntered into her bathroom.

A quick shower was followed by a laborious twenty minutes drying and styling her long hair. She walked back into the bedroom, but there was no sign of Alex. Hardly surprising, she thought, with a tiny smile playing around her mouth. The only occupation her husband lingered over was lovemaking, much to her delight. Everything else in his life he achieved with a speed and efficiency that left lesser mortals standing.

Lisa took her time. She slipped on a pair of cream lace briefs, and then, seated at the dressing table, she applied the minimum of make-up. She selected a cream soft cotton dress from the wardrobe, and slid her arms into its tiny cap sleeves. Pulling the edges together, she deftly fastened the tiny buttons down the front, from the low scooped neckline to the hem that flared out jauntily a few inches above her knees. Slipping her feet into a comfortable pair of cream canvas sandals and picking up a matching canvas shoulder bag, she surveyed her reflection in the mirror, flicking a long curl back over her shoulder.

'Very nice.' Alex appeared behind her.

Spinning around, a broad smile lighting her face, she bobbed a curtsey. 'Thank you, kind sir.' Her eyes roamed over him; dressed in black trousers and a black knit polo shirt he looked so vibrantly masculine she wanted to reach out and touch him, and he knew it.

His brown eyes darkened. 'I could give golf a miss and we could, perhaps, find something more interesting to do. Does the notion appeal?'

Any other day Lisa would have said yes, but not today. She was meeting Jed in London and they only had three hours together—not much for five years of friendship.

'Jake would never forgive you standing him up, and I have to meet my friend in London,' she said with a rueful smile.

'Forget I asked,' Alex drawled lightly. But his eyes glittered hard as they flicked over her. 'How are you getting there? I don't want you driving into London on your own. Get Bert to take you.'

'There's no need. I'm driving to the station and taking the train.'

'So be it,' he said curtly, and left.

What had rattled his cage? she wondered with a frown as she followed him downstairs a few moments later. Alex had been angry last week when he'd returned from golf. This week he was mad before he started! For a sport that was supposed to be relaxing it didn't seem to do much for Alex. Still, it was not her problem, though she winced as she heard the screech of tyres on the gravel drive…

The taxi stopped outside a large building, left over from the era of the grand London townhouses. This one had been converted into a modest hotel. Paying the driver, Lisa leapt out of the cab and ran up the steps. She walked between the two massive columns that supported the portico and into the hotel's foyer, and glanced around with interest. To one side was the reception desk, and in front a grand staircase, a couple of sofas and a table with a few magazines on display, across the wide hall an arch opened into a lounge bar. She still couldn't quite believe she was going to meet Jed in the flesh. She had his photo, and all his confidences, but meeting him after so long was a thrill.

Excited anticipation put a spring in her step as she walked into the lounge bar and glanced around. Apart from the barman, it was empty.

'Lisa, is that you?' a deep voice enquired, with a noticeable American drawl.

She turned, and a broad grin split her face. 'Jed!' She recognised him immediately—looking older than in his photo, and totally out of place next to the shabby but comfortable very English décor. He was tall, long-legged and narrow-hipped, his faded blue jeans fitting him like a second skin and his half-unbuttoned shirt seemed to be straining the remaining buttons over his massive muscular chest. His attractive face was tanned a deep golden brown, and was in sharp contrast to his sun-streaked blond hair. But it was his eyes that really captured Lisa's attention. Deep sapphire-blue, with a light of such piercing brilliance in their depths, they reflected a tenderness that could not be disguised.

For long moments they simply stared at each other.

'Damn, but you're beautiful enough to make a man change his mind, Lisa.' A deep tide of red surged up Jed's face. 'Sorry for the language.'

Lisa chuckled. Though a year older than her, it was good to know Jed could still blush. 'No apology needed,' she said, with a broad smile that illuminated her whole face. 'And you look like a cowboy,' she added, having noticed his boots.

Two great arms curved around her and swung her off her feet, and a deep chuckle rumbled from the bottom of his chest.

She clasped his neck and he gave her a great bear hug, before setting her back on her feet. 'A part-time cowboy, as you know.' He grinned down into her face, still holding her. Staring into each other's eyes, a look of complete understanding passed between the two of them.

'You have no idea how much your friendship means to me,' Lisa said, suddenly serious, her blue eyes filling with tears of joy.

His blond head bent and he pressed the lightest of kisses on the curve of her cheek. 'It works both ways. Without your support and understanding, I would never have got this far.'

Neither of them saw the tall, dark man standing in the archway observing the tender scene, but suddenly all hell broke loose.

Lisa stood rooted to the spot as Jed's arms fell from her waist and he went flying backwards in a blur of movement, to land flat on his back a few feet away. Caught off balance, he'd had no chance. Lisa stared in horror, at Jed's assailant: Alex! His dark eyes gleamed like the coals of Hades in the blank mask of his face as he stood over the floored Jed.

Galvanised into action, Lisa dropped to her knees beside her friend and tenderly brushed the hair from his brow. 'Are you okay? I'm sorry, so sorry.'

'Hush.' Jed managed a grin, and, leaning up on his elbows he added 'I'm fine.'

'How touching,' Alex grated, his lips drawn back against his teeth in a malevolent sneer. 'My wife and her boyfriend in a seedy hotel for a seedy affair.' He took a step forward, towards Jed.

Lisa, shaking with fury, leapt to her feet and grabbed Alex's arm, terrified he was going to grab Jed again. 'You great brute!' She didn't know how Alex had got here, or why. And she didn't care. 'Are you mad?' she demanded, her blue eyes flashing fire.

'Look, buddy you've got it all wrong. Let me explain,' Jed said, trying to cool the situation.

Alex turned to look down at the younger man, his black eyes pitiless. 'You want her, you're welcome to her.' And, turning on his heel, he walked out.

The colour drained from Lisa's face. She could not believe what had just happened. She closed her eyes and shook her head.

She felt the warmth of a protective arm around her shoulders and sagged against Jed, who was now back on his feet. 'Are you okay, Lisa?' Jed's husky tones got through to her.

Lisa turned her head to look up into his face and gasped, lifting her hand to stroke along his cheekbone, where the swelling was already evident. 'I should be asking you that. I can't begin to apologise.' She shuddered again at the image of Alex grabbing hold of Jed.

'Shh. It's okay. It takes more than that to anger me. My brothers have tried for years to get me going and failed.'

Lisa's lips quirked in a tiny smile; she knew what Jed meant.

'I guess that was your husband. Pity you didn't have time to introduce me; he seems quite a man,' Jed observed laconically.

'More beast,' Lisa answered, a desolation in her voice that she could not hide as the full horror of what had happened sank into her mind.

'Don't be too harsh on the guy. He loves you; that

much is obvious,' Jed sighed. 'I guess this is the end of our meeting. You better go after him.'

'Go after him? Never,' Lisa said adamantly, her shock giving way to righteous anger. 'He had no right to follow me, and no right to call me names, and he most definitely had no right to grab you, the savage swine that he is.'

'He was jealous, Lisa, give the guy a break. It's not all his fault. Did you tell him you were meeting me?' Jed asked quietly.

'I told him I was meeting a *friend* in London.' The more Lisa thought about it, the angrier she got.

'Anger is a waste of emotion, Lisa. And, be honest, did you actually tell him you were meeting a man?'

'Since when did you become my conscience, Jed?' she queried with a wry grin.

He grinned back, but didn't answer the question. 'He's your husband. Go after him and explain.'

She looked up into Jed's handsome face, so open and honest. 'No, Jed, this afternoon is for us. I don't know why or how Alex appeared like he did. But he is not going to spoil our afternoon together.' And, clasping his hand in hers, she added, 'It's a glorious day. We are going to have our walk in Hyde Park, sit in the Italian Gardens and take a boat on the Serpentine; everything I promised you.'

'If you're sure, Lisa.' The expression on Jed's young face was incredibly grave. 'But promise me when you get home you will explain to your husband the truth—that we're friends, nothing more.'

Lisa felt overwhelmingly protective of this man she had met for the first time today. She knew Jed had not a cynical or nasty thought in his head, money didn't interest him, only people, and he would never understand a ruthless predator of a man like Alex.

'Of course I will, Jed, and don't worry. Alex and I will be laughing about this by dinnertime.' Forcing a brilliant smile to her lips, she tightened her fingers around his calloused palm. 'Now, come on, cowboy, you can watch the horse riders on Rotten Row and tell me how they compare to Montana.'

At six in the evening, Jed helped her onto the train. She turned and leant out of the window, and brushed a gentle kiss on his tanned brow. 'Till the next time, Jed.'

His brilliant blue eyes glistened with something remarkably like tears. 'I've had a wonderful afternoon, Lisa. Never mind the rocky start. Know that I will always be there for you.' The guard sounded his whistle and the train moved off… Lisa waved until the platform was out of sight.

CHAPTER TEN

LISA stepped reluctantly out of her BMW just as the heavens opened. She walked up the stone steps to the front door to her home and got thoroughly soaked in the process. Great! Just great... That was all she needed.

It was only her promise to Jed to explain their relationship to Alex that had brought her back to Stoneborough tonight. Was she destined to be a fool all her life where Alex was concerned? She had forgiven his escapades with Margot and Nigel. She had even convinced herself he loved her. But his behaviour with Jed had finally shown her the truth. Alex did not love her.

How and why he had followed her today, she had no idea. But he was not talking his way out of this latest episode, she vowed silently. Much as she loved him, she had no intention of being a doormat for any man. Her pride would not let her. With her dress plastered to her body by the rain, she pushed open the front door and walked into the hall. She didn't see Alex until he spoke.

'I'm amazed you had the nerve to come back. Like living dangerously, do you?'

Her head lifted, he was striding towards her, wearing the same black pants and shirt he had donned for golf that morning. He looked incredibly sexy, and a wayward leap of her pulse told her she was not immune to him. But whatever game Alex had been playing today it certainly had not been golf...

Dropping her purse on the hall table, she shrugged. 'I live here, and I need to change.' A confrontation with

165

Alex was inevitable, but not yet. Because she knew if she did confront him now, her anger would get the better of her and she would say something she might regret. Brushing past him, she headed for the stairs, but he was faster than her and blocked her way.

'Don't you walk away from me!' he bit.

That was the last straw for Lisa. No way was any man going to talk to her like that, especially not an arrogant devil like Alex. She flung her head back, her blue eyes spitting fury. 'Get out of my way, you great brute, you Neanderthal numbskull,' she raged, swiping at him but missing, as he caught her flailing hand.

'A Neanderthal? A brute, am I? You dare to call *me* names?' An expression of cold derision tautened his handsome face. 'This from a woman who has spent the afternoon in the arms of her toyboy.'

'Don't be ridiculous! Jed is not a toyboy; he's a year older than me,' she snapped.

'And that makes your betrayal all right?' Alex enquired silkily.

'Betrayal?' she threw back, her eyes warring angrily with his. 'That's rich, coming from you. I went to meet an old friend, and what happens? You appear like some demented dervish, knock him flat, and whirl off. And *I* am in the wrong? Oh please…'

'What kind of fool do you take me for?' Alex rasped.

'The kind of sneaky, devious fool who spies on his wife because he thinks everyone's morals are as low as his own,' Lisa shot back hotly. 'The kind who conveniently forgets to retrieve the key of his apartment from his mistress.' She was on a roll and could not stop; she was so incensed by the injustice of Alex's attitude. 'The kind of man who thinks the only relationship between a man and a woman must be carnal.'

His hand released hers to snake around her waist and bend her back over his arm before she had a chance to move. He captured her mouth in a ravishing kiss. His mouth searched, teased and tormented with a devastating thoroughness, until she whimpered in despair at her own frailty and lifted her hands to cling to his broad shoulders.

'What happened Lisa?' he demanded softly, his mouth close to her lips and brushing sensuously over their swollen fullness. 'Tell me?' He kissed her eyelids and the small curve of her ear, and her hands with a will of their own slid from his shoulders to his nape, twining in his silky black hair. His kiss, his caresses plunged her into a sensual sea of need, which overrode all her good intentions.

His dark head lifted. 'No answer?' Lisa stared up at him in frustrated desire, not able to trust herself to respond.

'After cyber sex with your boyfriend, the physical reality a bit of a letdown was it?' Alex demanded mockingly. 'The young man not quite as experienced in the flesh, as you would have liked?'

The import of his words hit her like blows to the heart. She could not believe he could be so cruel. She stared at him. His dark eyes were as cold and hard as a block of ice. Her hands fell from his shoulders, her fingers curling into her palms, her nails digging into her flesh as she fought to control the agony of frustrated desire. What was it about him that made him irresistible to her? While she was tormented by aching passion, he was as contained and remote as Antarctica. A frozen waste—a very apt description of their marriage.

'You're disgusting,' Lisa said in a raw voice, but, worse, she disgusted herself.

His arm fell from her waist and he stepped back. 'Liar.'

His smile mocked her, his narrow-eyed gaze triumphant. 'I could take you now...'

Lisa went red, then white. It was one insult too many. She stared at him with bitter, hostile eyes. Tall, dark and strikingly handsome, but she must have been mad to imagine she had loved him. He didn't deserve to be loved.

'You're a stunningly sexy woman, Lisa, but I have never taken another man's leavings and I am not going to start now. I may have married you, but that is easily remedied.' He cast her one long, derisory glance. 'Pack your bags. I want you out of here within the hour. Anything you leave can be sent on to Stratford. My lawyer will be in touch next week. Personally, I never want to set eyes on you again.' Spinning on his heel, he crossed the hall into his study, slamming the door behind him.

Shock held her rigid. She squeezed her eyes tightly closed. Alex was throwing *her* out. The arrogance, the sheer hypocrisy of the man took the breath from her body. For a second rage engulfed her. She took a step towards the study, and then stopped. Alex was not about to listen to anything she had to say, and, in all honesty, she no longer had any desire to explain about Jed.

Alex did not love her, and never would. He was not capable of the emotion. Let him think she had betrayed him with Jed. He would anyway. This way at least she kept her pride. He would never know how much she loved him.

Several weeks later Lisa sat at her desk, fingering the pile of mail the office junior had just delivered. The recent past had taken its toll on her fresh-faced beauty: Her golden tan had faded, and deep purple shadows framed her large blue eyes.

Lisa picked up the first letter, a bill, and dropped it in

her in tray. Opening the next letter, she scanned it, her eyes widening in horror. As a major shareholder in Lawson Designer Glass she was requested to attend an extraordinary board meeting called by Xela Properties—in the other words, Alex—on Friday the twenty-third of September. The subject for discussion was the future direction the company should take. The meeting was scheduled for twelve noon in a private suite at a local hotel.

Lisa read the name and blanched. The same hotel in which her wedding reception had been held. She dropped the document on the desk and let her head fall back on the slender column of her neck, closing her eyes. Why was she surprised? She had been waiting for the axe to fall for weeks. Though she would not have believed one man could be so unrelentingly vindictive.

Moisture glazed her eyes, and she blinked hard. She was not shedding another tear for Alex Solomos. When he had thrown her out she had returned to live with Harold. The first night her anger had kept her going—but by the next she had cried herself to sleep. On the following Tuesday she had swallowed her pride and telephoned Alex at Stoneborough, only to be told by Mrs Blaydon he did not wish to speak to her, and all further communication between them must be conducted through his lawyer, Mr Niarchos.

Lisa had heard nothing more until a week later, when she had received divorce papers in the post. But once she'd read the divorce petition, she'd seen red... Any last lingering hope of reconciliation had vanished from her mind. All her old feisty spirit had returned... No way was she letting Alex get away with naming Jed Gallagher as the co-respondent in their divorce. If he wanted to play dirty, Lisa vowed she would do the same. She had instructed Mr Wilkinson to cross-petition, citing Margot. There had been an ominous silence ever since.

Wearily, Lisa brushed a few stray strands of hair from her brow, and looked once more at the document in front of her. Even knowing it was only a matter of time before Alex would make a move to dismiss her and put his own plan into action, it had still come as a shock. Alex had won. But then she had been naive to think she'd had a chance against the man. He was an arrogant, merciless adversary, a powerful man who always got what he wanted, and she should have recognised it the night she met him.

She recalled that first Sunday when she had gone out with him and when he had asked her to marry him. Then she had thought his proposal the most romantic thing in the world. But he hadn't asked, he had told her. She could hear his voice now. *'I am going to marry you, Lisa. You are going to be my love, the mother of my children.'* She had thought he was telling her he loved her. What a joke! He had recognised the overdue sexual awakening in her eyes and had used it for his own ends. He had secured a very lucrative business deal, and an innocent girl as his wife and mother of his children.

Alex was a throwback to the Dark Ages, a pure male chauvinist. His reaction when she had met Jed was understandable, given his flint-hearted nature. Like Caesar's wife, Lisa had to be above reproach, and the slightest hint that she was not, had been enough to cast her out.

The door opening broke into her bitter musing. 'Lisa?' Harold walked into the office and frowned. 'What's up? You look dreadful.'

Silently she handed him the letter and watched while he read it.

'Good, good.' He visibly relaxed. 'I'm delighted you're

going to meet Alex. I know he loves you. It's obvious this meeting is a ploy so you can get back together again.'

'You think so?' Lisa responded dryly. Harold didn't know about the divorce; she hadn't the heart to tell him. He thought they had just had a fight.

'Of course. It couldn't be anything else. He knows you hold the majority of shares in the company anyway.'

'Yes,' she lied. And watched Harold leave happily. She still hadn't told him about her donation to the hospice, and obviously neither had Alex when he'd convinced Harold to sell. Poor Harold would be devastated if he knew that by selling to Alex, he had destroyed any chance Lisa had of keeping Lawson's. Let him be happy for a few more days; he would know soon enough after Friday.

The scales had fallen from her eyes and she could see it all clearly. Alex had manipulated and deceived from day one. It wasn't enough for him that he had broken her heart; now he was intent on grinding her into the dust beneath his feet, along with Lawson Designer Glass.

But not necessarily... Lisa mused, the light of battle sparkling in her blue eyes. She spent the next half hour on the telephone to her lawyer. The following day she spent walking around Stratford-upon-Avon until she had found what she was looking for...

At five minutes to twelve, Lisa parked her car in the hotel car park and slid out. With trembling hands she smoothed the short black skirt of her fine wool suit down over her hips and adjusted the bright red collar of her blouse over the lapels of her tailored jacket. She had taken special care with her make-up, and had swept her long hair back off her face and into a knot on the top of her head. On her feet she wore black stiletto shoes coupled with sheer black silk stockings that accentuated the length of her legs.

Tightening her grasp on her briefcase, she walked into the hotel.

Lisa crossed to Reception, and enquired of the male receptionist directions to the Oberon Suite. He responded with a broad, admiring smile, and told her it was on the first floor.

Her stomach churning with nervous tension, she glided across the lobby, a tall, stunningly attractive and elegant woman, totally unaware of the admiring glances of every man in view.

Ignoring the lift, she ascended the stairs to the first floor. The Oberon Suite. Wasn't Oberon the king of the fairies in *A Midsummer Night's Dream*? she mused, as she walked along the wide hall reading the door signs. It hardly suited Alex's macho image, but she needed a touch of magic if she hoped to survive the next hour with her pride intact. She had to face Alex one last time and let him see she didn't give a damn!

Her eyes flicked over a name-plate and she stopped. Taking a few deep breaths, she lifted her hand and knocked firmly on the door; straightening her shoulders, she composed her face into a cool, polite smile and opened the door.

Two sofas covered in blue velvet were set either side of an elegant fireplace, at the other end of the room was a large rectangular table set with the accoutrements for a business meeting. But the model building placed in the centre of the table confirmed her worst fear: the proposed redevelopment, no doubt. Lisa moved into the centre of the room. She glanced again at the table, and as she did so a large black leather high-backed chair that had been facing the window suddenly spun around.

'You came. Brave of you. I had a bet with myself you wouldn't.' With the sun behind him she was not able to

see his face clearly, but it made no difference; she knew
that slightly accented voice as well as her own. It was
Alex…

'And on time as well. Would you like to take a seat
and we can begin?'

Her legs trembled, and it took an enormous effort of
will to walk to the table and sit down on the nearest chair.
'Good morning.' She gave the conventional greeting without looking at him, and, placing her briefcase on the table
in front of her, she clasped her hands tightly in her lap
and waited.

'As the only two shareholders, in what is really a family
business…'

Alex began to speak, and at his mention of 'family
business' Lisa's head jerked up, her eyes narrowing angrily on his dark face.

His black hair was longer than when she had last seen
him, but the tanned handsome face still wore the mask of
derision she remembered so well. He was enjoying this,
she realised bitterly. Not content with discarding her like
so much garbage, he wanted to watch her be destroyed.
Why else would he mention that Lawson's was a family
firm, other than to rub in her failure to retain it? Well, he
was not going to get away with it if *she* had her way.

His black eyes caught hers and she immediately looked
away, unable to stand the intensity of his gaze. 'I have
had my architect prepare a model to show you how we
envisage the finished complex.'

Lisa's glance skimmed over the model, but she didn't
see it. She wasn't interested.

'What do you think, Lisa?' The strident question had
her glancing at Alex once more. He was watching her, a
wary anticipation in his dark eyes. Why, she had no idea.
Alex knew damned well that she couldn't oppose him. In

fact, she had decided she was not going to try. She wouldn't give him the satisfaction.

'I think you've said it all. Do you want to go through the charade of taking a vote?' She could almost taste the tension in the air. The hairs on her neck were standing on end; it was sheer bravado that enabled her to hold his gaze. 'All in favour say aye,' she announced facetiously, and lifted her hand.

'Lisa, you haven't even looked at the model.'

'What's the point? You own Lawson's, have done for months. It's yours to flatten to the ground. I wish you luck with it.' Her gaze roamed over his perfectly chiselled features and she felt the beat of her heart quicken, knowing it was time to have her say and get out.

'The only reason I am here is to tell you I am prepared to sell you my forty-seven per cent stake at the same rate as you paid Harold. But, in return, I want the right to retain the name Lawson Designer Glass. So, do we have a deal?' she asked firmly.

His dark brows rose and she could see she had surprised him. 'Why?' Alex settled back in his chair, his narrowed eyes fixed on her face.

'Does it matter? You've got what you want—the land, the river frontage…that was all you were ever interested in.' She made no attempt to hide the edge of bitterness in her tone.

'You malign me, Lisa. Not a good idea when you are asking for a favour.'

'I don't want a favour from you. I want what is mine: my name.'

'I thought your name was Solomos.' The taunting softness of his comment made her anger rise. But she refused to give in to it.

'Not for much longer, and you know perfectly well what I mean.'

'Humour me. Tell me why.'

'I have found alternative premises for the glass foundry. I intend relocating and starting again. That way none of my employees need to suffer because I believed all your lies. They will all keep their jobs.'

'I might have guessed.' Alex's sensuous mouth quirked in a smile of reluctant appreciation. 'Very noble. But then you always were far too noble for your own good.'

'Not something you have ever suffered from,' she snorted, suddenly fed up with the whole mess. Pushing back her chair, she stood up. 'If you have no objections, I'll expect your lawyer to be in touch about the financial details as soon as possible.' And, picking up her briefcase, she walked round the table and headed for the door.

But she didn't get far. Suddenly she was stopped from behind and held against Alex's muscled length. The air whooshed out of her and she dropped her briefcase. 'Let go of me!' She was sick of playing the sophisticated businesswoman; she just wanted to get away.

To her surprise, Alex released her immediately. She bent down to pick up her briefcase, and before she had time to straighten up he had crossed the room and locked the door.

'What do you think you're doing?' she cried. Locked in a hotel suite with Alex was the last place she wanted to be.

'You will soon see,' was his enigmatic reply as pocketing the key card he walked towards her.

Lisa swallowed nervously. Suddenly what had appeared to be a large, elegant room at first sight now took on the proportions of a bird-cage as far as she was concerned. Her blue eyes skated warily over Alex. He was wearing a black pin-striped three piece suit, the jacket fitting perfectly over his wide shoulders; with a grey silk shirt and matching tie, he looked devastatingly attractive and infinitely dangerous.

He stopped a foot away from her, but he made no effort to touch her. There was a curious stillness in his stance. But his dark eyes strayed restlessly over her, from the top of her head to her toes, and back to her face. 'You're looking very beautiful, Lisa.'

'Thanks. But your opinion means nothing to me,' she said curtly. 'Open the door and let me out of here.'

'You really don't like me, do you?'

Like him? Her heart lurched. Not so long ago she had loved him more than life itself. 'No,' she snapped, banishing the unwanted memory from her mind. But just looking at him was having a disastrous effect on her senses.

'Are you afraid of me, Lisa?'

'No. I am simply surprised you asked me here at all. I distinctly remember you saying you never wanted to set eyes on me again.'

'I lied.' He smiled tightly, and his hand reached out, but she quickly took a step back, not wanting him touching her. She remembered the last time all too vividly. His hand fell to his side. ' How is Jed, by the way?' he queried softly.

'The last I heard, he was in Rome.' Alex had a nerve asking, but she refused to be riled, and answered him conversationally. 'He managed to E-mail me from an Internet café. He's due back in Montana this weekend.' But she could not resist adding, 'I might go and stay with him for a week or so while our lawyers work out the finer points of our deal.' Let Alex think she was going to her lover...

'I think not, Lisa.' He moved a step closer, and Lisa took another step back, and another until she bumped into the table. 'Because there is not going to be any deal. I am not buying you out, and I am keeping the trade name.'

Her face went ashen. For sheer malevolence Alex had no equal. 'You bastard!' she swore. 'Why did I ever marry you?' She shook her head. 'Our divorce can't come quickly enough for me.' Lisa had been functioning on adrenaline for the past half-hour, but suddenly the enormity of what had happened finally hit her. This man had taken her company, and now he was holding her captive. What more did he want? Her life's blood? She felt her knees weaken, and with Alex towering over her she was glad of the table to support her.

'No, we are not.' A black brow lifted and a ruthless smile slanted his sensuous mouth. 'Because I have decided to take you back. So stop playing games.'

Lisa's mouth fell open in shock. She was powerless to utter a word. He wanted her back! It didn't make sense.

'No more pretending Jed is your lover.' He lifted a hand and tilted her chin with his finger, his dark eyes intent on her face. 'I had Jed investigated. He is in his final year at the seminary and will very shortly become a priest. According to all accounts, he is only one step away from an angel, and according to his brothers he has never had sex in his life.'

Fierce colour flooded her cheeks, and she wasn't sure if it was because of the warmth of his hand on her face, or her sheer anger at his daring to investigate Jed. 'You didn't tell his brothers your disgraceful assumption?' she demanded, finding her voice. 'Jed had enough trouble convincing his family to allow him to study for the priesthood. The last thing he needs is you accusing him of adultery.'

'No, I didn't, but no thanks to you. You could have told me he was a priest.'

'I seem to remember you never gave me a chance,' she bit out.

'I'm sorry, Lisa. Forgive me.' Alex's hand dropped from her chin and he stood with his arms hanging loosely by his sides, an air of vulnerability about him that Lisa had never seen before. 'You can't begin to imagine how deeply I regret the way I behaved, but if you would just let me explain.'

'Why should I? You never afforded me that courtesy.'

'Because I love you, damn it! He forced the words out between gritted teeth, and for a second her heart stopped. Then she remembered.

'Now who is playing games?' Lisa prompted, willing her voice to remain steady. At one time she would have given anything to hear him say he loved her. But not now; it was too late. 'You married me for a bit of real estate, remember?' She declared, but it was more to remind herself. She was not falling into Alex's clutches again. Her marriage had been a rollercoaster ride to hell, and she wasn't paying twice. 'In fact, I seem to recall you telling me you did not believe in love. So what *are* you after, Alex?'

She was on the defensive. She couldn't help it. Her awareness of Alex was such that it was agony for her to be in the same room with him, and to compensate she lashed out, 'You already have my property.' She waved her hand in the direction of the model.

Alex visibly flinched. 'I deserved that,' he said with unnatural humility. 'But if you would only look at it!' He forced her to turn and face the model complex. His humility hadn't lasted long, she thought dryly.

The building was long and low, only four floors, with

gardens leading down to the river and to one side more buildings forming a courtyard. 'Lawson's.' She read the tiny blue lettering on the front of the model and fury enveloped her. 'You've called your hotel Lawson's?' she cried, spinning around and glaring up defiantly at his face, only inches from her own. 'Why did you do it, Alex? A sop to your conscience? But then we both know you haven't got one.'

'Even now, you really don't see, do you?' Alex asked flatly, slipping his arm around her shoulder and turning her back to face the table. 'If you look closely—' he stretched his other hand across in front of her, one finger pointing to the courtyard and the low buildings '—you are not going to lose Lawson's Designer Glass. The architect has incorporated the glass house, with a viewing area for the general public, into the overall design. So you see, you have nothing to worry about. It is quite common to have a few selected attractions in the grounds of a hotel.'

Stunned, Lisa stared down again at the model, her blue eyes widening in wonder, and then she lifted her puzzled gaze to Alex. 'But...but... Why...? I mean...' She stammered to a halt, completely gobsmacked.

Tentatively, he slid his hand to her waist and turned her fully to face him, locking his hands loosely behind her back. Lisa was too shocked to offer any resistance. 'I never thought I would see the day when I would bare my soul over a conference table.' His lips twisted in a self-mocking smile. 'But you deserve no less after the way I treated you.'

Baring his soul. A minute ago Lisa would have argued that the man did not possess a soul. She couldn't take it in. Lawson Designer Glass was saved. Alex was confusing her yet again.

'I know I have hurt you in the past, Lisa.' He'd got that right. The ache in her heart was a constant companion. 'But it was never my intention.'

Lisa swallowed nervously, unsure where Alex was leading. But deep down inside a tiny flicker of hope unfurled. 'No?' she queried.

'No. Believe that if you believe anything, Lisa. From the second I set eyes on you I wanted you,' Alex began in a deceptively quiet tone. 'But you were right; the night I met you in Stratford I was there to see Margot. Though only to tell her it was over. And I didn't spend the night with her. We had separate rooms.' His voice became cynical. 'But it did not stop Margot trying to persuade me into her bed. Which is why I never got the key back. I left in rather a hurry in the end.'

'I see,' Lisa said shakily.

'I hope you do.' Alex's eyes bored into hers, dark and oddly pleading. 'I could hardly wait till ten the next morning to see you. Then when we spent the day together, and I discovered you were feisty, and fun and yet innocent, I decided your credentials were perfect for a wife, and that I was going to marry you. I deliberately rushed you into it.'

That wasn't strictly true, Lisa silently acknowledged. She had been no slouch herself. She had wanted him and found it hard when he'd insisted they wait until their wedding night.

'I would like to say that business had nothing to do with it, but I want to be totally honest with you. I don't know.' His hands tightened behind her back, pulling her slightly nearer, as though he was frightened she would try to break away. 'When Nigel approached me at the bar, it might have crossed my mind that I could have the woman

I wanted *and* a lucrative business opportunity. But within a day of knowing you all I was interested in was *you*.'

She didn't know what to believe. He need not have admitted he hadn't been sure of his own motive that first night. Warily, Lisa tilted her head back and looked up at him. What she saw in the depths of his deep brown eyes made her heart skip a beat as warmth flooded though her veins, and she was tempted to give him the benefit of the doubt. His arms tightened a fraction more and her legs brushed against his, making her vitally aware of the electric tension between them. In a last-ditch attempt to control her crumbling defences, she murmured, 'But I did overhear you talking to Nigel.'

'Ah, yes, Nigel. When I came back from New York, and you knew I had bought the shares, everything I told you was the truth, Lisa. I did it to protect you.'

She had believed him at the time, but after Jed she'd been willing to discredit his every move. Now, after seeing his plan for the complex, she had to believe him again. 'I believe you,' she conceded, but she was still not sure where he was leading.

'Thank you for that.' He eased her into the hard heat of his body and pressed his mouth to her brow.

Lisa raised her hands and palmed them on his broad chest, whether in resistance or simply because she ached to touch him she did not know. She was powerless to utter a word. She felt as though she was on the brink of some great discovery.

'It is more than I deserve.' Alex's eyes caught and held hers. 'Because what I have to say now shows me in a very unfavourable light.' His sensual mouth turned down in a grimace. Lisa held her breath, the hope that was slowly growing in her frozen.

Alex kept an arm around her waist, and as though in a

gesture of comfort he lifted his other hand and caressed the soft curve of her cheek, his dark eyes kindling as he registered the slight dilation of her pupils. 'I had it all, and in my conceit, my arrogance, I did not know it. Of all the lovers I have ever known…'

Lisa stiffened imperceptibly. The last thing she needed was a rundown on his women. 'No, there were not that many, Lisa.' He read her mind with ease. 'But you were the most passionate, the most generous, giving… And I took everything you had to give and took it for granted.' His eyes clouded with what looked suspiciously like remorse. 'I could make excuses. I did not believe in love because of my parents. My mother loved my father, still does, but would not forgive what she saw as a betrayal.'

Lisa suddenly saw the parallel in their relationship. Alex had caught her in the foyer of a hotel and had thrown her out of their home. He was more like his mother than she had thought, and she listened with mounting hope as he continued.

'But that is the easy way out. In reality I had reached the age of thirty-five without experiencing the emotion, and was cynically convinced it did not exist. Until I met you. But even then I refused to recognise it.'

Her blue eyes widened to their fullest extent on his serious face. Was he implying again that he loved her?

'Even after the fiascos with Margot and Nigel were sorted out and we went to Kos…' Their eyes met and clung for a long moment with memories shared. 'Even then I could not admit to myself that I loved you. In my conceit I didn't think it mattered, because I knew you loved me. On our honeymoon, you delighted me with your unabashed enthusiasm, both physically and verbally. But after I returned from New York it slowly dawned on me you no longer said the words. You became a silent lover. I told myself it did not matter, but it did,' he admitted with a self-mocking smile.

Alex was right; she had withdrawn slightly, out of insecurity, but she hadn't thought he'd noticed. The hope expanded to every part of her as he went on.

'I found myself growing more and more suspicious. I was jealous of the time you spent E-mailing your friends. Then, on the night I got back from Singapore, I went into your study to get the fax from the pottery chap.' Pain clouded his expression, and involuntarily Lisa's hands stroked comfortingly up over his chest.

He gave her a crooked smile. 'I found a printout of an E-mail with the address of a hotel in London and it was like a knife in my gut.' He paused. 'I have absolutely no excuse for following you, or grabbing your friend Jed. It was sheer rage, primitive male jealousy; the man was touching my woman.' He said it with such possessive arrogance Lisa had to mask a smile. It was so Alex… He could not remain humble if he tried.

'In that moment I knew the sheer agony of love and betrayal.'

'Not betrayal,' Lisa interjected swiftly.

'You were close to Jed mentally. Is a betrayal in the mind any less harmful than a physical betrayal, Lisa?' he asked, and she did not know how to answer him. His eyes never left her face as he bent his head, and brushed her lips gently with his own. 'Forget I said that. Just know I love you, Lisa. I think I always have, but I was too arrogant to admit it,' he murmured against her mouth.

'But you still insisted it was over…'

'Hush, Lisa.' Alex lifted a finger and placed it over her lips, and she marvelled at the slight tremor in his touch. 'I will regret to my dying day the way I behaved. You are my wife, and I will love and treasure you in this world and the next, if you will let me.' His dark eyes gleamed with the fierce burning light of love. There was no mistaking it, and Lisa's lips parted in a brilliant smile of pure joy, her shimmering blue eyes reflecting the love she found in his. 'Will you?' He repeated huskily.

Lisa had a million questions to ask, but they could wait. Swaying towards him, she moved her hands up to his wide shoulders, and then trailed her fingers through his hair, bringing his head down to hers. 'Yes, I will. In fact, I will insist,' she teased, and placed her lips on his. Delicately probing with her tongue, she initiated a kiss that was tender and passionate, loving and giving, a kiss like no other they had shared. Finally, so he would be in no doubt, she looked up at him through her thick lashes and murmured, 'I believe there is a bedroom next door. It would be a shame to waste it. After all, you have paid for it, partner.'

Alex's husky laugh contained an element of relief, and he bent and curved an arm beneath her knees and lifted her high against his chest. 'Your wish is my command,' he groaned, as her hands slid around the nape of his neck and she nuzzled his neck.

They fell on the bed, clothes discarded haphazardly, and finally, when they were both naked, Alex reared up over her, his eyes dark and feverish as they roamed over her slim curves and the luscious fullness of her breasts. 'I do love you, Lisa.' She felt her breasts grow heavy beneath his gaze.

'Then love me,' she whispered, and he did…

MILLS & BOON®

Presents...

MARRIAGE BY DECEPTION *by Sara Craven*

When Ros met Sam Hunter on a blind date, she thought they were the perfect match—if only she hadn't been pretending to be someone else…

A VENGEFUL REUNION *by Catherine George*

Leonie has been working abroad since breaking her engagement to handsome property developer Jonah Savage. Now, he is the first person she meets upon her return! Secretly, Leonie still loves him, but does Jonah share her feelings?

THE ULTIMATE SURRENDER *by Penny Jordan*

When Polly's husband died, his cousin, Marcus Fraser, offered her a home, a job, and himself as surrogate father to her baby. But Polly had to fight her attraction to him, certain that his affection stemmed only from family duty. And then he kissed her…

MISTRESS BY MISTAKE *by Kim Lawrence*

Handsome Drew Cummings had misjudged Eve, believing her to be a calculating seductress in pursuit of his wealthy nephew. So when Drew seemed intent on seducing Eve himself, was he simply protecting his family fortune?

Available from 7th April 2000

Available at most branches of WH Smith, Tesco, Martins, Borders, Easons, Volume One/James Thin and most good paperback bookshops

0003/01a

FREE
4 BOOKS
AND A SURPRISE GIFT!

We would like to take this opportunity to thank you for reading this Mills & Boon® book by offering you the chance to take FOUR more specially selected titles from the Presents...™ series absolutely FREE! We're also making this offer to introduce you to the benefits of the Reader Service™ —

★ FREE home delivery
★ FREE monthly Newsletter
★ FREE gifts and competitions
★ Exclusive Reader Service discounts
★ Books available before they're in the shops

Accepting these FREE books and gift places you under no obligation to buy; you may cancel at any time, even after receiving your free shipment. Simply complete your details below and return the entire page to the address below. **You don't even need a stamp!**

YES! Please send me 4 free Presents... books and a surprise gift. I understand that unless you hear from me, I will receive 6 superb new titles every month for just £2.40 each, postage and packing free. I am under no obligation to purchase any books and may cancel my subscription at any time. The free books and gift will be mine to keep in any case.

POEC

Ms/Mrs/Miss/Mr ....Initials ....
BLOCK CAPITALS PLEASE

Surname ....

Address ....

....

....Postcode ....

Send this whole page to:
UK: FREEPOST CN81, Croydon, CR9 3WZ
EIRE: PO Box 4546, Kilcock, County Kildare (stamp required)

MILLS & BOON®

Makes any time special™

The
Australians

Passion's Mistress *by Helen Bianchin*
Seven years ago Carly, unknowingly pregnant, had
left Stefano Alessi when she discovered he had a
mistress. Now settled in Sydney, her daughter is
desperately ill and needs expensive care. There is only
one person Carly can turn to for help. Stefano…

One Fateful Summer *by Margaret Way*
After sixteen years apart, Shelley and her father are
together again. But her father's partner, Raf Conway
thinks she's just after her father's money. Shelley
can't tell Raf the truth—so after this summer will
she ever see him again…?

Heart-Throb for Hire *by Miranda Lee*
Kate, a successful Sydney career woman, didn't think
she could attract a man. So when Roy Fitzsimmons
burst onto the scene Kate was suspicious. Surely such
a sexy guy couldn't have feelings for her?
Just what was he playing at?

Look out for The Australians in April 2000

0003/05